TRAIL TO SUNDOWN

Even badmen occasionally ride with dreams, and Jerry Lannigan's dream had been to come back to the town of Sundown to claim Gay Houseman as his bride.

Jerry had to be tough: his father had died when he was a youngster, and he had been shipped out to work for an old man. And now he was further embittered and hardened by the news that the girl he had come to seek had not waited for him.

But Jerry was needed in Sundown—both to protect the property he had inherited, and to safeguard the very life of the man who had moved in as its tenant . . .

TRAIL TO SUNDOWN

Barry Cord

First published by Foulsham

This hardback edition 1999
by Chivers Press
by arrangement with
Golden West Literary Agency

ISBN 0 7540 8048 X

British Library Cataloguing in Publication Data available

Printed and bound in Great Britain by
Redwood Books, Trowbridge, Wiltshire

TRAIL TO SUNDOWN

CHAPTER 1

The two riders pulled up at the rim of the valley. They had broken camp at dawn, and though it was not yet nine o'clock, they had put four hours of trail behind them.

This far they had come from the Mexican border, a matter of eight days travel; only one of them would continue north, following a little used road to the Wyoming town of Guerra.

The older man settled in his saddle, easing cramped leg muscles. The valley held no meaning for him—he had gone past the age where sheer grandeur of country stirred him. Tiredly he reached inside his coat pocket for the makings while his eyes passed over the wild, rock-jumbled country directly below the valley rim to the far thread of river glinting in the morning sun. Barely visible, a town made its pattern in the distance.

The younger man stretched forward over his saddle horn, eagerness riding his voice. "That's it, Judge. Home."

The older man brought his limp cigaret to his lips and leaned to strike a match across his saddle. He was amused at the younger man's tone. He cupped his hands around the flame, his eyes sombre.

"You won't stay," he murmured. "Things change in five years. Especially women."

The younger man turned impatiently. He was a compact, muscular man whose age was deceiving. Crisp blue eyes, curly brown hair and a small pug nose hammered slightly out of line gave him a boyish look. He was twenty-five.

"Some things change," he said confidently. "But not the valley of the Jay. Not Gay."

"Judge" Jenkins smiled cynically. The "Judge" was an appellation he had received as a result of the finality with which he dispensed "law" from the muzzles of the long-barreled Colts that rode holsters tied down snug against his sinewy thighs—not from any formal election to office. It was doubtful if Jenkins had ever looked into a law book, or any book—he was not the reading type.

But in fifty years of living he had come to understand a great deal about men—and women. The good and the bad, and the in-between. And he felt sorry for Jerry Lannigan.

"I'll be waiting in Guerra for yuh, son."

Lannigan studied this man, irritation pinching his mouth. He and Jenkins had been together for three years, since the day they had teamed up to nail down the law in the tough border town of Salinas. What he had learned from this hard man he could never repay. But suddenly he resented the older man's cynicism.

"It'll be a heck of a long wait!" he snapped.

Jenkins shrugged. "If you say so, kid."

Jerry smothered the quick rise of his temper. "Ride down with me, Judge," he invited. "See what a peaceful town is like for a change."

Jenkins shook his head. He chuckled mirthlessly. "It might spoil me, kid."

Jerry's voice came through tight lips. "Then drop by on your way back to the border. When you do, stop at the H Bar H and drink a toast to a happily married man."

Jenkins took a long drag on his cigaret before flicking the butt over the rim. Then he swung his cayuse away, heading back for the trail to Guerra. Jerry stared after him, anger flooding through him, darkening his face. But the older man softened his abrupt departure. A hundred paces away he looked back.

"I hope she's still waiting, kid. Good luck."

It was past noon when Jerry reached the Little Jay, a shallow trickle that slid like quicksilver over the white gravel of the stream bed. His dusty roan horse stopped of its own volition, thrusting a lather-flecked muzzle into the water.

Jerry let the animal drink. The sun beat down on his back, burning through the thin protection of faded blue cotton shirt and underwear. Half-moons of sweat showed under his armpits.

He let his eyes take in the wild country across the stream, forgetting that once he had been impatient to leave. Remembering now only the bright patterns of his boyhood when, a ragged, half-wild youngster, he had followed every game trail, explored every savage ravine, known every rock-jumbled ridge in this grim strip of territory called the Crescent. For thirty miles this region of poor grass and stunted growth flanked the richer bottomlands of the Jay. Through this gullied, unwanted land threaded a dozen obscure and narrow trails that faded and lost themselves against the high red wall that flung a savagely protective arm around the northwestern curve of the valley.

The Crescent had a bad name, and inevitably the aroma of its reputation attached itself to the gentry who lived in it. A few scattered homesteads lay within its inhospitable confines, occupied by close-mouthed men who had nothing in common with the valley ranchers and little with each other.

The scolding of a jay in a clump of junipers wiped the older memories from Jerry. He had grown up in the Crescent. He had been seven years old when his ailing, widowed mother farmed him out to Jed Lafreau. She had died the following year.

He retained few memories of her, none of his father. But he remembered Jed, a stiff, untalkative, reserved man who had kept him on—let him grow with a minimum of restraint.

What had brought Jed Lafreau to settle in the Crescent, Jerry never found out. Like the others who eked out a living in that jumbled land, Jed was a close-mouthed man. He seldom went to town; he received no mail. But he was the only father Jerry Lannigan had known.

Sitting there, with the jay scolding him from the junipers, the sun hot on his shoulders, Jerry remembered Jed. A small, dark man with bitter black eyes, his form shapeless in weathered bib overalls, a greasy black square-crowned hat tilted back over sparse gray hair. A stub of a cheroot which he never smoked jutting from the corner of his mouth.

Five years ago, Jerry reflected. He had told Jed

his decision to leave the night before, and the next morning, his few personal belongings rolled in his war bag, he had gone out to the barn to saddle his cayuse. Jed had followed him, the bone-handled Colt he always wore sagging the cartridge belt around his thin waist.

He leaned against the barn wall, watching Jerry saddle.

"You won't find it, son," he had stated calmly.

Jerry turned. "Find what?"

"Whatever you'll be looking for, outside." Jed had a way of speaking, Jerry remembered, that was half insult, half mockery—and always bitter.

"I'm not looking for anything," Jerry had replied stubbornly. "It's just that I'm tired of riding the Crescent— I want to see some of the country beyond the Wall."

"Yo're letting them run you out, kid," Jed had sneered. "Yo're letting them sanctimonious sons down in Sundown run you out—"

"No one's running me out," Jerry had cut in roughly. But in a way, now, he knew he had lied to Jed. He had grown up in the Crescent, and he had been unwanted down in Sundown. At the Saturday night dances the mothers had frowned as he approached their daughters; the older men had eyed him with unfriendly regard. From the sheriff Lafe Stevens down to the lowliest swamper no one—except Jed, and Gay Houseman—had been sorry when he left.

Jed had eyed him broodingly. "Come back, then," he said quietly, "when you're ready." He slid gnarled fingers down to the Peacemaker on his hip, slipped it out of holster. "Yo're young an' hotheaded," he stated laconically. "Trouble's mebbe the first thing you'll find out there. Take this—" he tossed the gun to Jerry, who caught it, surprised by the suddenness of the offering. "Remember what I taught you. Don't lay a finger on that handle until you mean to use it—then shoot straight. And good luck to you, Jerry."

That was the way, Jerry remembered, that he had left the Broken Circle. . . .

His parting with Gay Houseman had been different. He had met her under the Cathedral, a rock spire on the edge of the Crescent, seven miles from Big Tom Houseman's H Bar H. Jerry had met Gay there before. She had reddish brown hair that tumbled down over her shoulders, full red lips that often curled petulantly, gray-green eyes that teased.

"I'll wait for you, Jerry," she had said. "I'll wait for you—forever!"

Five years was a long time. But it was not forever.

"Come on, Rebel," he said impatiently, pulling the roan's muzzle out of the water. "We'll ride in on Jed first and surprise the old coot."

The roan splashed across the stream and lunged up the sandy bank. A hundred yards farther on they ran into a faint trail and Jerry turned Rebel south, remembering that this trail would bring him past the Homer place. Lee Homer he remembered as a stringy, white-haired man who had run a few goats on a quarter-section of arid land.

Jerry heard the dog's wild barking before he came in sight of the shack. It was a sharp, staccato yelping that broke off into a whimper, only to break out again, racking the hot stillness with an undercurrent of horrible frustration.

Jerry was frowning as he broke through a clump of scrub oak and emerged into a stony clearing.

A sun-warped, weathered board shack squatted in the pitiless heat of the sun. Between the shack and the open-fronted shed that had served Homer as stall for his goats a big brindle dog cowered in the clearing, whimpering softly. Six feet of rope held the animal captive to a stake driven firmly into the hard-packed earth.

The dog was the only living thing present. The house was empty. Most of its windows were cracked or gone altogether. Wind had built a ramp of fine sand to the threshold and scattered a thin layer into the room Homer had once occupied. Now its emptiness stared back at Jerry through the open doorway; the whimpering dog only accentuated the loneliness of the place.

Jerry rode slowly to within a dozen feet of the animal before dismounting. The brindle crouched, its whimpering changing to an ominous, rattling growl in his throat. Jerry frowned. Blood streaked the animal's gray-brown coat. A wicked gash over the dog's left eye seeped blood that still glistened in the sun.

Jerry's spine tingled. It suddenly occurred to him that someone had been beating this animal only a few moments before he had ridden through the scrub oak!

But the small, miserable spread that had belonged to a man named Homer seemed deserted. Jerry turned a puzzled gaze to the shed, let it drift past the small rock corral that had once penned Homer's goats. Finally he turned his attention to the dog.

"Someone had it in for you, eh, boy?" he queried softly. "Heard me coming and hightailed it—"

But he wasn't sure. Suddenly he felt that cold prickling down his spine again, and he cursed silently, sweat chilling on him. Whoever had been engaged in brutally beating this helpless animal had not left. He was somewhere out in that rock jumble beyond the corral, watching Jerry. . . .

The animal backed away from him as he moved forward, its fear-laced warning rumbling in its throat. Jerry paused. A three-foot length of oak, split from a sawed chunk of firewood, lay at his feet. Tufts of blood-matted hair clung to one end.

Jerry's flesh crawled. The silence in the yard was intense. Again he felt the sudden nameless prickling down his back, as if someone were sighting down the ominous length of a rifle at his back!

Jerry's jaw tightened. His Colt was out of immediate reach in his saddle bag—a concession to the orderly peace of Jay Valley—and a reaction to nearly five years of living with it within easy reach of his hand.

Now he felt nakedly exposed in the glare of the sun beating down over that bare, deserted yard. A man who could find pleasure in beating a dog would have little compunction shooting a stranger in the back!

He forced himself to bend down, pick up the club. He had to act as though he were unaware of the hidden rifleman; instinctively he felt the uncertainty in the man would immediately crystallize to murder if he made a sudden wrong move.

The dog backed away from him until the rope stopped him. His mouth opened, but now he made no sound. Small red eyes watched him.

Jerry said softly: "I won't hurt you, boy. See?"

He tosseed the club away. The brindle followed the flight of the bludgeon. Jerry hesitated. The animal probably weighed sixty pounds and it would put up a mean fight if it felt cornered. But he couldn't let it remain here, exposed to the punishing sun.

He reached inside his pants pocket for a clasp knife. "I'm going to cut you loose, boy," he muttered. "You can go home."

The dog crouched. Jerry kept talking. His voice sounded strange in that empty yard. He reached out and caught the rope. The brindle snarled. Black, blood-flecked lips writhed away from white fangs.

"This won't hurt a bit!" Jerry reassured tightly. "See!" He drew the blade quickly across the rope. The animal lunged back. The rope parted and the brindle sprawled backward. It recovered swiftly, made a quick half-circle around Jerry, then streaked for the timber. A foot and a half of rope still dangled from its collar.

Jerry straightened. The sweat beading his face was not entirely from the heat. And then he became aware of riders heading down into the pocket —riding toward him. Two men he had never seen before. But he was immeasurably grateful for their appearance.

For the ominous prickling at his back had left him!

Watching the newcomers, it occurred to Jerry Lannigan that the Crescent had changed since he had left it. Men like Homer seemed to have given way to a more ominous breed. A breed Jerry recognized—he had run into them along the Mexican border. Tall or short, they were stamped by the same calling—a calling that ran to violence, that respected only the fastest gunhand!

He had observed the change in the manner of their riding the moment they saw him. A slight shift of posture, a quick interchange of glances. That was all, but it conveyed a lot to Jerry Lannigan who, with "Judge" Jenkins, had marshaled some of the craggiest towns along the Mexican border.

They came into the clearing, curbing their dusty cayuses a few feet from him. The older man, tall and rawboned and chewing tobacco, slouched carelessly over his saddle horn, yellow eyes raking Jerry with insolent appraisal. The absence of a visible weapon on Lannigan puzzled him.

"Stranger?"

Jerry shrugged.

The man brushed the back of his right hand across his tobacco-stained mustache. "You thinkin' of settlin' here?"

"Might."

The younger gunman was short, wiry, narrow-shouldered. He had pale, pale eyes and blond hair that was bleached almost white. He didn't look older than twenty—a dangerous man, Jerry thought, because he hadn't yet learned what it was like to look into the muzzle of a faster gun.

"Talkative cuss, ain't yuh?" the youngster

sneered.

Jerry looked at him coldly. "That bother you, son?"

The gunster flushed. The older man's chuckle sounded in the stillness. "He's got you pegged, Whitey, for shore." He turned his attention to Jerry, dropping a hand carelessly over the handle of his Colt. "Hate to head yuh off this way, fella," he said falsely. "But this place happens to belong to Nate Beals. We work for him."

"What happened to Homer?"

The older man exchanged a quick glance with Whitey. "Never heard of the gent," he said sharply. He eyed Jerry with sudden suspicion. "Thought you said you were a stranger here?"

"I didn't say anything," Jerry answered coldly. "You've been doing most of the talking."

Whitey sidled his mount between his companion's and Jerry's. "Let me handle him, Davis," Whitey rasped. He was standing stiff-legged in his stirrups, his fingers curling eagerly around the handle of his Colt. "A slap across his mouth with this—"

"Shut up!" Davis ordered harshly.

Whitey eased back into saddle, sullenness pinching his mouth.

Davis jerked a horny thumb at Jerry's patient roan. "You better climb aboard, fella, before you get hurt. If yo're smarter than you look, you'll keep on ridin'. Clean out of the valley!"

Jerry nodded. Temper had pushed him this far, but discretion faced the grim facts. The two men confronting him were armed, he was not. He turned and lifted himself up into the roan's saddle.

Whitey suddenly edged his fidgety mare close. Davis' rebuke was galling him and he was not used to it.

"This'll help you along!" he snarled. He lifted his Colt free in a sudden jerk and backhanded Jerry across the face. The unexpectedly vicious blow rocked Lannigan's head back; he felt his cheek split by the metal impact. Blood made a warm path down his face.

He reacted instinctively. His fingers closed around the gunman's wrist, jerking the hand down in a violent twist. Whitey screamed as bones cracked in his wrist. The Colt made a heavy smash of sound between the two riders. Both animals parted violently.

Jerry's fingers were still clamped around Whitey's wrist, and as the animals separated he jerked Whitey out of his saddle. He made a lucky grab for Whitey's Colt as the gunman sprawled face downward on the hard-packed ground. The man landed hard.

Jerry swung erect, kneeing the roan around. He held Whitey's Colt in his left hand, the muzzle challenging a slack-mouthed Davis.

"I'm ambidextrous," he informed the tobacco-chewing gunman grimly. "If you don't believe me, try making the mistake he did."

Davis closed his mouth. Then he shook his head. "I'm not makin' any mistakes, fella. Whitey had it comin'." He glanced down at his stunned companion. "Probably busted his nose," he commented callously. "I reckon that makes you even."

Jerry wiped blood from his cheek with the back of his right hand. "I didn't come here looking for trouble," he growled. He kneed his roan to Davis, held out Whitey's gun. "Give it to him later," he advised briefly. "But tell him to keep out of my way."

He turned the roan away and rode out of the small clearing, not looking back.

CHAPTER 2

Jed Lafreau's Broken Circle spread straddled the Upper Jay, a small clear stream that began with springs that bubbled up from the base of the Wall. Low ridges covered with juniper hemmed in the small green valley; at the eastern end of the small basin they came together to form a funnel through which tumbled the Upper Jay. A wagon trace followed the stream through this gap, finally joining the H Bar H road to town.

The Broken Circle was the one spread in all of Crescent's thirty miles that was worth anything, and Jed Lafreau had guarded it jealously. Several times Houseman riders had come to the gap, looking for strays, only to be turned back by the bitter-eyed man who rode with ready shotgun.

Jed Lafreau had been in the valley ten years before Jerry went to live with him and yet he remained a stranger. He bothered no one, seldom went to town. He was a self-sufficient man, content to live within himself. He ran a few cows to keep him in beef and pocket money, he kept some chickens and he found relaxation in a truck garden. Ambition, if he had ever been nagged by it, had long since been laid to rest.

Yet he was not a placid man, nor had he always been content to lead such a life. Once, within Jerry's memory, he had received a letter. It had been from Virginia, and it had been penned in a woman's hand. Jed had read it that evening, his face showing a strange torment in the lamplight. Then he had torn the letter and fed it to the flames in the wood stove. He had sat up the rest of the night, drinking; during the early morning hours Jerry heard him stumble into bed.

He had slept late that next day. But when he got up he had made no mention of the letter, nor had he acted as if he had ever received one. Nor did he ever write in answer, if answer had been called for.

This was the man who had raised Jerry Lannigan—and in a way he typified the Crescent. . . .

The drowse of late afternoon hung in the air as Jerry swung the blowing roan way from the wagon road, seeking a familiar and shorter way into the small basin. The roan threaded through the junipers on the ridge and came down the steep slope, splashing across the shallow Jay. A quarter of a mile upstream the Broken Circle's familiar stone and log house basked in the westering sun.

A dog's sudden barking startled the roan. It minced high, turning warily to eye the canine that came racing out of the thicket upstream. Jerry ran his hand soothingly along the roan's arched neck. "Whoa!" he muttered. "Looks like our friend, Rebel—the fella we cut loose back at Homer's place."

It was the same brindle. Someone had cut the trailing rope from its collar and washed the blood from his muzzle. It occurred to Jerry that anyone who could do that had to be on pretty friendly terms with the brindle, and he wondered if Jed, in his loneliness, had taken to a dog.

The brindle planted its feet on the bank and barked again, head cocked a little to one side. This time his bark had a questioning note, as if he had recognized the man on the horse.

Jerry grinned. "You lost, fella? Or—"

"It's not Buddy who's lost," the girl said tartly. "But it looks as if you might be. Or perhaps you never learned to read!"

He swung around, surprise flushing his face. The girl had come down along the brush flanking the stream. She looked like a boy in belt Levis and blue shirt, except that she filled these items of apparel in places no boy would. She had a young, pert face and Jerry would have placed her at about seventeen or eighteen, except that her eyes had a more mature look.

She repeated her question, her voice sharp. "Can't you read?"

"Read what, ma'am?" he asked agreeably.

"There's a sign posted at the entrance to the valley," she snapped. "You must have passed it."

He shook his head. "Came in over the ridge—

always came home that way," he added as an after-thought. He became aware then that the brindle had stopped barking. And another figure had come to stand beside it on the bank.

The boy was about ten, Jerry judged. A wiry, leggy, dark-haired boy with an unfriendly face. He carried a .30-30 Winchester in his brown hands and he seemed quite capable with it.

The girl noticed him, too. She called sharply: "Tommy, put that rifle down!" There was a trace of fear in her voice.

The boy obeyed without comment, without haste. He slid the Winchester butt down by his bare feet. His face remained watchful, unfriendly, beneath his battered straw hat.

Jerry said dryly: "I didn't know Jed had rela-tives, ma'am."

The girl looked at him, frowning. "As far as I know," she said, "he didn't."

Jerry shrugged. Movement upstream caught his eye and he lifted his eyes to the house where a tall, spare-framed man in white shirt and string tie was coming at a rapid walk toward them. The man was a stranger to Jerry.

"When I left here five years ago," he explained to the girl, "an old codger named Jed Lafreau lived here. I came back to pay him a social call, ma'am."

"We live here now, mister," the boy said. He had a thin, challenging voice; it was as unfriendly as his eyes. "Jed's dead."

Lannigan murmured: "Sorry—I didn't know."

Five years, after all, was a long time. Some of the eagerness that had ridden with him from the border ebbed. And his parting words to Jenkins came back to irritate him with their unreasoning assurance.

Jed Lafreau was dead and someone else had taken over the Broken Circle. He gazed soberly at the slim, pretty girl, at the unfriendly boy, at the dog eyeing him silently now, ears pricked alertly— and shifted his glance to the tall man hurrying toward them.

A suspicious people, he thought soberly. Perhaps the Crescent bred unfriendliness in its occupants.

He touched his hat brim with the tips of his

fingers. "Sorry if I've bothered you," he said quietly. "I didn't know Jed was dead."

The tall man had reached the girl's side. He looked at Jerry with an anxious expression that was somewhat relieved when he noticed that Lannigan was not wearing a belt gun. The man had a long thin face ravaged by worry. It was a scholarly face, smooth-shaven, emotionally soft. It was not the face of a rancher or a farmer. Jerry wondered what had brought this man to settle in the Crescent.

"You one of Nate Beals' riders?" the man asked worriedly.

Jerry shook his head. "I just rode. by," he explained again. "Used to live here when Jed Lafreau owned the place."

The man's pale blue eyes shadowed. He licked his lips and glanced at the girl. "Jed's dead," he said tiredly. "We bought this place from the county clerk, down in Sundown, six month ago."

Jerry nodded. All at once the familiar scene seemed strange—there was an air of inhospitality about it that cut the edge of his homecoming.

He turned his attention to the dog, knowing

that he was dragging on his stay here and yet not knowing why. The weight of the long miles, unsustained now by the eagerness which had buoyed him, settled wearily over his muscled frame.

"I see the dog got home all right," he remarked.

The boy brought the rifle up into his hands, his voice sharply querulous. "Buddy just came home, mister. Beat up, and a rope around his neck. What do you know about it?"

"Not much," Jerry answered. The boy was eyeing him with sharp hostility, not minding the girl's sharp order to put his rifle down this time. The man's voice joined the girl's, but his tone had a beaten quality that indicated he did not expect to be obeyed.

"I ran into Buddy at the old Homer place, about nine miles north, near the Little Jay," Jerry explained. The boy and the dog, he could see, were close, and there was something wild and unbridled in the youngster that struck an oddly familiar note in Jerry. For a moment he seemed to get a glimpse of himself, fifteen years back in time. . . .

"He was tied to a stake in the yard," he went

on carefully, judging the temper in the boy's eyes. The girl was splashing across the stream, her attention now wholly centered on the stubborn youngster. The older man had ceased his remonstrances.

"I cut him loose, about four hours ago," Jerry added. He noticed now that the boy's eyes seemed fixed on his face, and he remembered the dried streak of blood on his cheek and that the boy had possibly misinterpreted it. Instinctively he raised his hand to the stiff cut.

"I had a little trouble at Homer's," he said dryly. "After Buddy left."

Tommy's mouth was a thin slit. "Buddy was gone all right," he said thinly. "What were you doing—"

The girl reached his side, grasped the rifle. "Tommy!" She did not try to tear it from the boy's grasp, and after a brief moment of hesitation the boy let her take it from him.

Jerry said: "Thank you, ma'am."

The tall man said: "Tommy meant no harm, stranger. It's just that"—he looked across the Jay to the girl and boy—"we've been having trouble lately," he finished. He made a worried gesture with his hands. "Someone's been after the little stock we have. Twice someone's fired, after dark, through the windows of the house."

His gaze lifted to Jerry, and the younger man saw in him a worried, uncertain man out of his environment, unable to cope with the violence that seemed to have become part of the valley of the Jay.

"My name's Henry Akers," the tall man went on. "That's my daughter, Marion—and Tommy. My wife's an invalid. We came here hoping to take life easy—all we want is peace. I thought—"

The girl cut in sharply: "He's not interested in our troubles, Dad." She was standing by her brother, the rifle held across her slim waist—and it came to Jerry that if Henry Akers was a misfit here, his children were not.

"Guess Jenkins was right," he murmured. "Things have changed." He touched fingers to his hat brim again. "I'm sorry I bothered you, Akers," he said quietly.

The brindle barked once, questioningly, as Jerry

turned the roan back to the wagon road that led
out of the basin.

Big Bill Houseman's H Bar H lay between the
Crescent and Sundown. It was a long ride to
Houseman's spread, and a farther one to town—
and Jerry decided against riding in to the H Bar H
at night.

He made camp at the edge of H Bar H range,
close by Cathedral Rock where he had often met
Gay. The stars hung low in the warm sky. He
tried to recapture the old familiarity. But he had
been away five years, and the stars over Cathedral
Rock were no different from the stars that clustered over the border desert. The events at
Homer's, the fact of Jed's death, had undermined
his image of the valley of the Jay—his plans had
been based on a mental picture he had refused to
believe would ever change.

He busied himself methodically, trying to shake
a dark moodiness that seeped into his thoughts.
This was home, he told himself stubbornly; this
was what he had come back for.

Jed was dead. And it looked as though there were trouble in the valley. But there was still Gay. He had ridden over a thousand hills in five years; he had lost the insular feeling of his boyhood. He had spent his restlessness against time and space; unshakably now he knew he had come back to the valley of the Jay to settle down, to sink his roots.

The roan shifted restlessly in the shadows beyond the fire he had built. Lannigan listened. A coyote wailed his grievance to the gibbous moon poking over the eastern ridges. It turned Jerry's thoughts to the brindle crouched in Homer's yard —and to the two men who had ridden down to claim the tumbledown spread.

Nate Beals' men, they had said. And Henry Akers, too, had asked if he was a Beals rider.

He tried to fit the man into this new pattern of trouble. Nate Beals, he remembered, had taken over his father's mercantile business just before Jerry had left the valley. He was several years older than Jerry—a handsome, self-assured man who had been confident of his place in Sundown. Taller than Jerry, and inclined to heaviness.

But Beals had been essentially a townsman. His roots were in the world of trade, of social contacts; he dealt with cloth and business houses with an Eastern address.

Why had such a man taken to hiring gunmen? What had prompted Beals to take over the Homer place? In all this it seemed to Jerry there was a false note. Homer's tumbledown shack had no apparent value.

But the coyote's wailing struck a chord of wariness in him. He reached out and slid old Jed's Peacemaker out of his saddle bag. He fell asleep with the Colt by his side.

He was up with the sun, and after a breakfast of cold beans washed down with the juice of his last can of tomatoes, he headed for Houseman's H Bar H. A worn cartridge belt cinched his flat stomach. Jed's old Colt lay snugged in the thonged down holster on his right hip.

To the casual eye Jerry Lannigan had changed little from the youngster who had left the valley five years before. He had filled out a little, mostly through the chest; his face still held its boyish cast.

The sandy stubble on his jaw and cheeks would have to wait until he got to a barber. But he had put on a clean shirt and clean pants, and his coat, slightly wrinkled, fitted easily over his wide shoulders.

He had left the valley with less than seven dollars in his pocket; he was returning with over seven hundred. He had saved that in the past year, when he had made up his mind to return. It would be enough, he thought, to stake out his own quarter-section and get married.

Two hours of steady jogging brought him out of the worst of the Crescent. Ahead of him the country sloped away to the river bottoms; beyond the glinting Jay the far eastern wall of the valley was a hazy blue backdrop. North of him the Jay narrowed, spilling finally out to the flat country past Paler's Peak.

For a long moment Lannigan enjoyed the view, seeing it through the clear eyes of a man who had been away long enough to feel the nostalgia of homecoming. . . .

The roan snorted impatiently, and he leaned

over to stroke the animal's muzzle.

The bullet ripped cloth from his coat sleeve, just above his elbow. Lead made a dark splotch on the boulder ten feet ahead of him, its whining ricochet making an angry sound in the stillness.

The faint crack of a Winchester from upslope told Jerry, as he wheeled the roan for the protection of rocks, that the rifleman was a long way back up the slope. But even as his roan passed between two protecting boulders, lead snarled off the nearer one, bringing a sudden tightening of Jerry's lips.

The second rifleman, he thought grimly, was nearer—and shooting at him from a different angle.

Lannigan flattened out along his saddle.

The roan kept going, keeping the boulders between him and the riflemen. Jerry heard one more shot. But it was wide, and the rifle crack was fainter, indicating that the men who had taken pot shots at him were not in the frame of mind to follow him.

Jerry slowed the roan's pace. That first shot, he reflected bleakly, had come almighty close. But they hadn't followed him, which in itself puzzled Lannigan.

Those shots might have been intended merely as a warning. A blunt warning to Jerry to keep riding—clear out of the valley!

Lannigan reined in and looked back. The rocky slope broiled under the rising sun. Nothing moved.

Lannigan's mutter was bleak: "Looks like things have changed in the valley, Rebel. Seems to be crowded with hardcases with itchy trigger fingers." A cold grin spread across his blunt face. "Maybe it's time someone tells them they're riding the wrong range, eh, Rebel?"

The roan, used to his rider's comments, made none of his own. He settled down to a steady jog again, and an hour later they hit a well defined road leading to the H Bar H. Soon after the ranchhouse loomed up. Jerry leaned forward, excitement beginning to throb in him.

The old cottonwoods still shaded the big yard, and the thought came to Jerry that this was a comfortable spread—not pretentious, but well kept and cleanly functional.

A quarter of a mile from the ranchhouse the road was barred by a pole gate. Jerry pulled up, frowning. The gate he remembered, but not the two riders who levelled rifle muzzles at him from the other side of it.

"Goin' some place, stranger?" the tall rider asked bleakly.

Jerry let his glance go past the man, to the house under the big oaks. "I thought this was the H Bar H," he said. "Big Bill Houseman's spread."

"It is," the rifleman said tonelessly.

Lannigan shifted slightly in saddle. "What's the idea of the hardware?"

The tall man glanced at his partner. The other shook his head. "Reckon you'll have to mosey along, fella. We've got orders—"

He didn't finish. He glanced past Jerry as a rider came up the road. He was a slim figure dressed in range clothes, a khaki brush jacket over narrow shoulders. The man came up to the gate, holding his blaze-faced black to a walk. A scowl pinched his narrow, good-looking face as he looked at Jerry.

Lannigan grinned. "Neither one of us have changed that much, Bob. Though the last time I remember you, you were just starting to scrape the fuzz from your chin."

Bob Houseman's scowl faded. He edged his cayuse up close, disregarding the frowning men on the other side of the gate. "Well, I'll be hanged!" he said simply. "Jerry Lannigan—the bad boy from the Crescent!" He stuck out his hand and Jerry took it.

Bob's handclasp was quick, nervous. He had a thin, sensitive face darkened by the sun, and it came back to Jerry that Bob looked like Big Bill the least of the three Houseman children. He had been a quiet, sober youngster not given to physical exuberance. But the years had put their change on Bob, too—his eyes had a bitter, go-to-the-devil look, and Jerry could smell the liquor on his breath from where he sat. The Colt jutting from a strapped-down holster, too, was an odd note.

Lannigan said casually: "The H Bar H has made a few changes since I was here last. I remember when even a Crescent man would be treated like a human."

"Seems like a long time ago, Jerry," Bob murmured. He looked at the men behind the pole gate. "It's all right, Belk. He's a friend." He waved his left hand, and the tall rider leaned over and unhooked the pole gate. He held the leather thong in his fist as he backed his cayuse, swinging the gate open.

Bob made a sweeping gesture with his left arm. "Come on up to the house," he invited. "Dad'll be glad to see you."

Jerry shrugged. There had been a time, he observed dryly, when Big Bill Houseman had not been glad to see him.

CHAPTER 3

A little of the old excitement gripped Jerry as he rode with Bob up the tree-shaded road to the ranchhouse. He had come up this way only once before—the night he had driven Gay Houseman back from Tom Bedlow's wedding. They had come up the tree-lined road with the moon filtering through the branches above, and he had been young and reckless and not caring. That was the night Big Bill Houseman told him never to set foot on the H Bar H again. . . .

A slim, hard-eyed man wearing two guns stepped out from the wagon shed as they rode up. He stood wide-stanced, eyeing Jerry with cold appraisal.

Bob caught Jerry's frowning regard. He said shortly: "Dad's taken on a lot of new hands lately. Most of them have been picked because they can handle a gun."

They rode past the gunman, reining in before the ranchhouse. A wide veranda fronted the yard. Honeysuckle hid the pole supports, filling the morning air with its heavy scent.

Bob Houseman took a deep breath. "The H Bar H, Jerry," he said. His voice had a forced gaiety. "There were buffalo in the valley when my father built his first sod shack here. The Housemans were here first, Jerry—remember that! They settled the valley, and they laid out Sundown. The Housemans have run the valley of the Jay now for twenty years—and come hell or high water they'll continue to run it!"

Jerry was hardly listening. He was looking up at the door, wondering if it would be Gay he would see.

Bob's slightly thickened voice beat loud against Jerry's ears; it was as though the man had to get something off his chest.

"Life is full of odd quirks, Jerry. Who would have guessed, a year ago, that a clothing store clerk would be bucking the H Bar H? And all because my sister turned him down!" Bob's voice was thick with bitter laughter. "A little thing, a man's pride, Jerry—but because of it the valley's become an armed camp, Sundown's split down the middle— imported gunmen swagger down the streets." He made a grimace. "You've come back just in time, Jerry. The valley's been building to the biggest blood-letting since the Civil War."

He was interrupted by the opening of the ranch-house door. A man bulked in the doorway, surveying them.

Jerry Lannigan's smile had a grudging admiration. He had found everything else in the valley changed, but not Big Bill Houseman. The rancher filled the doorway, his heavy-boned frame solid as granite. His broad, leather-colored face had been chiseled by sun, wind and weather, but will and stubbornness had moulded it. Over fifty, his tawny hair was only barely dusted with gray. Bright blue eyes, as clear as glass chips, challenged them.

Then the long iron slit of mouth under the heavy, straw-colored mustache curled. "Why, I'll be a jumping horned toad! Jerry Lannigan!"

Jerry grinned. "That's the first natural sound I've heard since I've come back, Bill."

"Light an' rest yore saddle, son," Big Bill growled. "Bob, see thet his bronc's taken care of. Come on in, son," he added. "I want to talk with you."

Jerry slipped out of saddle and let Bob take the roan's reins. In young Houseman's face was bitter irony. "Another gun for the H Bar H," he murmured, and left Jerry standing at the foot of the veranda.

Lannigan hesitated. The big man on the veranda was looking after Bob, contempt plain on his face. Something in Jerry rebelled then. "Bob!" he called out after the man. "Don't bother unsaddling Rebel. I won't be staying long."

Big Bill was frowning as he gripped Jerry's hand. "Never thought I'd be glad to see you, son," he said bluntly. "You were a wild one. Fact, I kinda drew a long breath when I heard you had left the valley."

Jerry said levelly: "I didn't expect to be welcomed back, either, Bill." He grinned a little wryly. "Last time I was here you made it pretty plain I'd never be welcomed—"

Houseman dismissed the incident with a brush of his hand. "You were a cocky boy," he growled. He ran an appraising eye over Jerry's compact frame. "What brings you back?"

Jerry hesitated. He wanted to tell this man that it was his daughter who had brought him here. But Big Bill went on, not waiting for his answer. "Guess you heard about Jed, eh?"

Lannigan frowned. He was beginning to realize that there was something connected with Jed's death he had not taken into account.

Big Bill was turning, shoving his door open. "Come on in, Jerry," he boomed. "Gay should be back soon. She'll be surprised to see yuh." He turned his head to Jerry and grinned broadly. "I used to think she'd gone sweet on yuh. But I guess she's got over it. She's out ridin' now with a young attorney from town—gonna marry him, she tells me." He made a gesture with his arm. "Grab a chair, son—I'll fetch a bottle out of the kitchen."

Jerry didn't accept the invitation. He stood in the middle of that big living room, only vaguely conscious of Big Bill's departure. Gay's mother was dead, but a woman's hand had arranged this room, lightened the sombreness of heavy oak furniture.

Lannigan didn't move. He was thinking of Gay, remembering the teasing smile on her full lips as she had murmured: "I'll wait for you, Jerry—forever!" And superimposed on this picture, distorting the image he had carried with him for five years, he saw Jenkins' hard, cynical features as he had said: "Things change in five years, kid—especially women!"

Houseman came in from the kitchen, bringing a bottle and two glasses. He glanced at Jerry's face, scowled. "It's all right, son," he misinterpreted Jerry's stiffness. "I don't give a hang what you were five years ago. The truth is, I can use a man like you now." He set the bottle of bourbon on the table and poured stiff jolts into small tumblers.

He handed Jerry a glass. "I got together a hard crew, son. I need a man tough enough to handle them!" He didn't even turn his head as Bob entered; he went on as if his son were not present.

"I've whelped two sons, Jerry! One's got no guts! The other hasn't the brains of a dumb ox!" The rancher lifted his glass to his lips and tossed the bourbon down.

"Yo're a valley man, son. An' you could always handle a gun. I'll give you two hundred a month to boss the bunch of hardcases I hired!"

Jerry forced himself to listen. "You're way ahead of me, Bill," he said. "What's happened since I left?"

"Trouble!" Big Bill growled. "Started a year ago. You remember Nate Beals—took over his father's store in Sundown when the old man died? Beals took a shine to Gay—started riding out here steady. Gay liked him, but—well, you know Gay, Jerry. When he got serious she turned him down,"

The old rancher snorted and poured himself another jolt. "Darn fool took it to heart. Started a lot of talk about Gay thinkin' she was too good for him—"

Bob Houseman's softly ironic tone cut across his father's explanation. "No one in the valley has ever been good enough for Gay, have they?"

Big Bill's head lifted then, his eyes bright with unconcealed contempt. "Shut up!"

Bob's face colored; hate made its momentarily livid pattern across his thin face. He had been standing by the door, like a stranger in this house that was so clearly dominated by the big man in the chair. Now he shrugged, smiled crookedly as he walked across the room, and disappeared through the far archway.

Houseman turned to Jerry. He went on as if the incident had never happened, as though his son had never been in this room.

"Beals tried to force himself on Gay, about a year ago. Darn fool was drunk. Gay was in the wagon with me—we'd just pulled up before Gray's General store." Big Bill brushed the back of his hand across his mustache. "I used the whip on him. Laid him up for a week, I heard."

He reached for his glass, brooded briefly over it. "Two months later he sold his father's store an' bought out Lorrenger's Lazy L. He's been spreadin' out since, hirin' gunmen. He's got friends in town. They've sided with him. Two of my men were cornered by a bunch of Beals' gunmen in a saloon across the river. One was killed—the other told to get out of the valley."

Big Bill heaved up out of his chair. "I've run this valley for thirty years, son. No dry goods clerk is gonna run me out. That's why I want you to stay. I heard some of the stories that came back about you from the border. I need a man like you here—"

Jerry shook his head. "Thanks for the offer, Bill," he said tonelessly. "But I won't be staying."

The rancher's eyes held a sharp disappointment. "Why, kid, if two hundred isn't enough—"

"It's not money," Jerry said. "But this doesn't look like my fight. Sorry."

Houseman frowned. "But—I thought when you showed up here—"

"I was paying you a social visit," Jerry cut in flatly. "That's all!" He raised the tumbler, took the bourbon in one raw, bitter swallow.

"Thanks for the drink, Bill."

Big Bill Houseman's face held sharp contempt. "Well, you had yore drink," he sneered. "What's holding you?"

"Nothing," Jerry murmured. He turned and headed for the door. He didn't want to see Gay. He didn't want to see anyone. Jenkins had been right after all. Everything had changed in five years—and he was a stranger here.

He stepped out onto the veranda in time to see them ride into the yard!

She was laughing, spurring up ahead of the man who rode somewhat stiffly behind her. They came almost to the house before Gay Houseman noticed the man on the veranda. She was riding a big bay horse with the natural grace of a girl who'd grown up in the saddle.

Dust kicked up under the bay's hoofs as he stiff-legged to a halt. She swung broadside, the laughter dying in her throat. For a long moment she stared at Jerry, her mouth making a surprised pout.

"Jerry!" Her voice was surprised—and confused. "Why, Jerry Lannigan!"

To the man watching from the veranda, she had changed little in five years. She dressed more formally now, he noticed, in a soft white silk blouse that caressed the swell of her bosom, a fawn-colored riding skirt. At eighteen she had been seen more often in faded jeans and one of her brothers' shirts, yellow hair tied in a horsetail with a piece of blue calico.

Her companion pulled up alongside. Dark eyes raked Jerry with dispassionate interest. He was a tall, slender man with dark sideburns that framed a rather hard, smooth-shaven face. He was a carefully groomed man, a self-contained man of thirty, and though he had obviously ridden in from Sundown, a matter of some eleven miles, he showed little sign of travel wear.

He slid down from his saddle and turned to Gay with the possessiveness of a man sure of his feelings. "An old friend, Gay?" he murmured.

The girl swung away from him. "Jerry—when did you get back?"

"This morning," Jerry said. He tried to make his voice casual. "Just dropped by—to say hello."

"Oh!" Gay paused, suddenly remembering the man behind her. "Walter—this is Jerry Lannigan. A boy I used to know."

Walter nodded. He stood by his cayuse, lifting a tailored cigaret to his lips.

Gay's smile was uncertain. "Jerry—" She pouted suddenly. "Jerry—it's nice seeing you. Come in. Dad'll be glad to see you—"

"I've seen your father," Jerry interrupted brusquely. He was holding himself, stiffening against the bitter hurt inside him. "He told me you were getting married!"

Gay's eyes were suddenly alight with teasing laughter. "Why, Jerry!" She walked to him, laughter tinkling in her throat, teasing him softly, reminding him sharply of what he had come back for. "You needn't look so hurt! I didn't expect you'd ever—"

Her eyes were mocking him, daring him. Instinctively he reached out for her, pulled her to him. She didn't resist. Her face lifted up to him, still laughing, and he kissed her, stilling her laughter beneath his rough lips.

Ten feet away Walter stiffened, his dark face registering a strong protest of outraged impotence.

Jerry let her go. Gay's eyes were dark, still teasing. "Stay awhile, Jerry—"

Lannigan brushed past her. He didn't look at the man who was going to marry Gay. His roan was tied by the water trough under the oak; he jerked the reins loose and swung aboard.

He didn't look back.

Belk was swinging the gate open for a thick-shouldered blond boy when he pulled up. Jerry swung aside, his glance brushing over a broad, pushed-in face, thick lips, heavy body. Vaguely Jerry recognized this youngster—Dab Houseman, Big Bill's youngest boy.

Jerry nodded grimly as he rode past.

Dab Houseman reined aside. He stared after Jerry for a long time, his small gray eyes narrowing, his thick lips pursing at some hidden thought.

He reached down to touch the stock of his Winchester speculatively; then he grinned broadly as he turned his cayuse up the road to the ranchhouse.

Belk watched him through cold eyes. Slowly he leaned forward to spit over his bronc's ears. It was a deliberate gesture of distaste.

CHAPTER 4

Sheriff Stevens leaned back in his chair, feeling old and tired. According to the battered alarm clock on his desk it was a few minutes after two. But already the day seemed overlong. He glanced at the papers on his desk. There was work he should have attended to. But he couldn't bring himself to it.

He sat and looked at the wall with unseeing eyes. After a while he got to his feet and walked to the door.

The law office fronted on River Road. From where he stood he could look up and down the tree-shaded length of Sundown that sprawled on the south side of the Jay. An old town by western standards—a town that had grown without haste, in peace.

From where he stood he could see the newer town, too, sprawling in haphazard pattern across the river. The wooden bridge spanning the Jay connected the old section of Sundown to this squalid, dingy cluster on the north bank; it also marked where the law ended.

In the old days the section across the river had been settled mostly by Mexicans and Chinamen, most of whom, he had suspected, were "wetbacks" who had drifted up from the border. They had performed the servile labor of the town, and the trouble they gave him, generally of a domestic nature, had been something he had easily handled.

But in the past year a newer and harder element had come to the "new town." A gun-toting, hard-lipped crowd that took over the two saloons in the area, raised their own brand of hell, and made their own law.

Some of them, he knew, rode for the Lazy L.

But not all of them were gunmen who had been hired by Beals. The sheriff suspected there were some who had been drawn to the valley by the impending trouble—hard men who hoped to gain by the range war brewing between the Lazy L and the H Bar H.

Unconsciously Stevens dropped a horny palm over his walnut-handled Colt. He was a tall, bony-framed man of forty. A bachelor, he had found being county sheriff to his liking, and over the years he had expended more genial effort in personal politics than in vigorous pursuit of law and order. He had been a good-natured sheriff, and he had had two young deputies who had not minded doing most of the hard work.

It was unfortunate that, in this period when he needed them most, one of them had been killed in an argument with a drunken homesteader. The other—? Lafe Stevens swung his attention to the corner where Ma Jennings' boarding house loomed over the street.

Brad was late, This morning, of all mornings,

he had expected his deputy to be in early. . . .

It was a peaceful afternoon. Birds sang in the thickets down by the river. A summer drowse hummed in the air, warm and benign, and Stevens cursed Big Bill Houseman in a sudden fit of temper.

He and Big Bill had been friends, until the incident that had turned Nat Beals from a respectable townsman to an unheeding, revenge-bent fool. Since that day the valley of the Jay had seen more trouble than he could handle. He had warned both men, in blunt terms, and Beals had laughed at him, sneering at his threats.

"Stay out of this, Stevens!" Nate had rasped. "I'm going to break Houseman—drive him out of the valley. I'm going to take everything he owns— even his daughter!"

"Whose side are you on?" Big Bill had bellowed. "Hang it all, Stevens, if you had any sense you'd have jailed that big-mouthed son long ago!"

Both men were stubborn fools, Stevens thought wearily. Now the valley was like an open powder keg, waiting only for an incident to touch off an explosion that would destroy it.

And all because of a light-headed woman! Stevens shook his head. No woman was worth it. But he knew that Gay Houseman did not entirely explain Beals' hate. Some men had a stubborn, deep-rooted pride—

The slamming of a door up the street disturbed his thoughts. Ma Jennings' twelve-year-old boy came down the steps in one jump and started at a run for the law office.

Even before he reached Stevens the sheriff knew something had gone wrong. Young Jimmy had a folded sheet of letter paper in his fist.

"Brad said to deliver this to you after two o'clock," the boy said. "He left town this morning. Gave me four bits before he left, too."

Stevens unfolded the note. He read the penciled words twice, something crumbling inside him. A cold knot formed in his stomach. He looked down at Jimmy and nodded, his smile tight and forced on his lips.

The boy's voice was curious. "You gonna cross the bridge, Sheriff?"

Stevens reached out and rumpled the boy's tawny hair with an absent-minded gesture. Then he turned and went back inside the office. He stood by the desk, looking at the alarm clock. But he wasn't noticing the time. He was thinking back to the threat he had made to Nate Beals last night —the promise that by sundown today he and his deputy would be over to close the Lone Star Bar if Beals did not turn over one of his gunmen before that time.

The Lazy L rider who went by the name of Link Ellers had come across the bridge yesterday, swaggered drunkenly into Charley's Saloon and, after being served whiskey, proceeded methodically to blast every bottle behind the bar. When Charley protested, Link had shot him through the stomach.

There had been half a dozen witnesses to identify him. But Link had a reputation as a gunman, and no one interfered. He had gone back across the bridge, and later, when Stevens had started after him, he had been stopped by Beals and several of his riders.

The sheriff sagged down in his chair. He had made his promise to Beals, knowing as he said it that it was an empty threat. But the showdown had had to come; the time had been reached when either the law meant something in Sundown, when it extended across the bridge if need be—or it had come time to turn in his badge.

He looked down at the note again. The message was short. *"Reckon I am yellow, Lafe. When you read this I will have left town. Sorry—and good luck. Brad."*

Slowly the sheriff's fingers crumpled the note. "Sorry," he murmured. He felt nausea rise in him. He let the balled note fall under his feet and walked back to the door.

He knew the bars along River Road were posting odds that Link Ellers would go free, that the law wouldn't have the guts to go across that bridge after him. The sheriff felt suddenly very old, worn out. He knew that if he had any sense he wouldn't cross that bridge at sundown.

A rider came up the street from the H Bar H road, and the sheriff thought for a moment it was one of Houseman's men. Then his glance steadied on the solid figure and his gray-shot eyebrows arched in thin surprise.

He whistled softly. "Jerry Lannigan!" He watched the newcomer ride slowly along the street and finally turn into the Sand Point Bar hitchrack. A stubborn sneer lifted a corner of his hard mouth.

"Wonder whose side you're on?" he growled. And with the speculation he knew that it didn't matter—that the trouble in the valley was already too far gone. He went back to his desk, settled his gaunt frame into the chair. Slowly, with great deliberation, he drew his Colt out of his holster and began to clean it. . . .

Jerry Lannigan paused by the hitchrack, dropping the roan's reins over the sun-bleached bar. He turned and glanced up the street where he had glimpsed Stevens' lanky figure, watching him from the law office door. But the lawman had gone back inside.

The afternoon burned the dust of the road, and under his coat he felt sweat trickle down his back. It had been a long ride in from the H Bar H, and neither he nor the roan was in the mood for more riding.

He patted the bronc's sweat-streaked hide. "I'll take care of you as soon as I get the dust out of my throat," he muttered.

He ducked under the rail and went up the saloon steps. The batwings creaked under his palms. He stopped inside the room just short of the door, his eyes adjusting to the dimmer light. He was conscious of eyes turning to him, of tension that picked up intensity swiftly, stilling even the far murmur of conversation at the end of the long bar.

Jerry thumbed his hat up from his sweat-beaded forehead. The bar had not changed in his absence. The same large oil painting of a plump nude hung over the bar mirror, flanked by two small and incredibly bad depictions of *Custer's Last Stand*. But most of the men lining the counter were strangers.

The bartender moved toward him as Jerry put his hands on the counter. The skin of his face and neck hung in loose, creased folds. He stopped across from Lannigan, frowning.

Jerry said: "I haven't changed that much, Joe. Or have I?"

Joe Semper spread his hands along the bar and leaned forward for a closer look. "I'll be hanged! It's Jerry Lannigan!" He extended a moist hand across the counter. "Didn't recognize yuh right off," he admitted.

Jerry grinned. "Had to look twice myself before I tabbed you. Last I remembered, you tipped Casey's scales at over two fifty."

Joe belched softly, smothering the sound against his palm. The gesture was habitual. "Stomach," he explained briefly. "Hurts all the time." He turned and selected a bottle from the shelf behind him. "On the house, Jerry," he said generously, pouring.

He shook his head at Jerry's invitation to join him. "Had to cut it out," he confided in a lowered voice. "Drinkin' milk now." He made a wry face.

Jerry lifted his glass. "Here's to a quick recovery," he said solemnly.

Joe nodded. "Glad to see you back, Jerry. You heard about Jed?"

It came back to Lannigan then that there was more to this statement than what had first occurred to him. He had assumed Jed had died of natural causes. Now he wasn't sure.

"I heard Jed was dead," he agreed levelly. "Heard the news for the first time last night when I rode up to the Broken Circle and found a family by the name of Akers living there." He pushed his glass toward the bottle and automatically Joe Semper refilled it.

"But I haven't heard how he died," Jerry suggested grimly.

Semper shrugged. "Someone clubbed him to death, about six months ago," he said bluntly. "I thought you got the news—"

He didn't finish, but Jerry knew what he meant. He thought Jerry had come back to the valley of the Jay to find Jed's killer. Slowly Lannigan digested this latest bit of information.

He had run into surprises from the moment he had entered the valley, and his mind had not yet adjusted itself to the changed situation. He felt whipped, drained, and he found that even Jed's killing failed to move him.

There was nothing here now that he wanted. In the morning he'd head out of the valley—and with the thought he pictured Jenkins' surprise when he rode into Guerra. Well, he had been wrong about the valley—and about Gay.

He finished his second drink.

Joe looked at him, crooking his head curiously on his left shoulder. "You staying?"

Jerry shook his head. "Leaving in the morning. Heading for Wyoming." His glance caught symbols soaped on the lower corner of the mirror. "Odds 3-1." He made a gesture toward it with his chin. "New game, Joe?"

Semper shrugged. "There's close to two hundred dollars in a cigar box on that shelf. All of it money bet against the sheriff." He turned and plucked a clean glass from behind him and scowlingly poured a small drink from Jerry's bottle. He downed it in one quick swallow and closed his eyes. He didn't look at Jerry when he opened them.

"I'm the only man in Sundown coverin' the odds against the sheriff," he muttered. "But Stevens always treated me right—"

Lannigan placed a double eagle on the counter. "I never got along with Lafe, in the old days," he said. "But I'll take a piece of those odds, Joe." He slid the gold piece toward the surprised barman. "What's the sheriff bucking?"

The men nearest him along the bar turned curious faces. The batwings creaked on dry hinges as a man pushed through. He joined the group at the far end of the bar. "Brad left town this morning!" he announced loudly. "I just got the news from young Jennings. Turned in his star and quit!"

There was a murmur among the customers.

Semper pushed Jerry's gold piece back to him. "Keep it," he suggested. "No sense bettin' against a sure thing."

Lannigan was curious. "What's the sheriff bucking?" he repeated.

"Beals," the barman answered. "Nate Beals—an' more than half a dozen craggy gunslingers Beals has brought into the valley." He filled Lannigan in on what had happened.

"You just heard about his deputy, Brad," Semper finished. "That leaves Stevens alone." The barman lifted his shoulders. "He'll never go across that bridge now."

"He'd be a darn fool," Jerry agreed. He finished another drink. The liquor was beginning to loosen his tired muscles. "Thanks for the drinks, Joe," he said. "Maybe I'll be back to treat you—some day."

He left the bar. He was at the doors when Joe's voice stopped him. "Jerry! You forgot somethin'." He was holding the double eagle between his fingers.

Jerry shrugged. "Put it on Stevens," he said, and went out.

The sun was halfway down in the sky. He blinked against the glare. A small spring wagon came churning up the dust in front of the saloon. He got a glimpse of the girl on the seat, holding the reins. A big brindle dog and a brown-faced boy shared the seat with her.

He tipped his hat to the girl and Marion Akers nodded acknowledgment. The dog barked in recognition, but the boy kept a stony face.

Lannigan shrugged. He stepped down to the hitchrack, untied the roan, and climbed into saddle. "We'll be out of here by morning, Rebel," he said, and the animal nodded vigorously, as though the decision pleased him.

He turned the roan in at the town livery stables and crossed the street to the barbershop. The money he had saved to get married on was burning a hole in his pockets. He got a haircut and a shave and spent a luxurious half hour in the zinc tub in the back room.

Clean and refreshed and the whiskey still warm inside him, he made his way back up the street to the two-story hotel that looked out over the Jay. He ordered steak and trimmings in the dining room and then, feeling oddly satisfied, he registered for an overnight room.

But he didn't go upstairs. He walked out to the broad porch where half a dozen men were seated in wicker chairs, watching the street. The sun's glare had softened; across the Jay the shadows were beginning to lengthen.

The man nearest Jerry sucked softly on his pipe.

A sudden wave of contempt swept over Lannigan. These men were waiting to see what Stevens would do. They were waiting for a man, alone in a hot office up the street, to make his decision. A decision that, whether they knew it or not, would affect all of them. But no one was offering to help.

The man at the far end of the hotel porch took a sudden breath. "Well!" he exclaimed sharply. "Looks like the sheriff isn't going to wait until sundown!"

Jerry's gaze slid along that dusty street, to the gaunt man who came through the law office door. The sheriff had tucked a double-barreled shotgun under his arm. He came down the steps and headed toward them, toward the bridge lying across the Jay.

Jerry thought grimly: He's got nerve, anyway, and in that moment he understood Stevens. The man had lived with his star too long to run out on it.

He settled back against the hotel wall, remembering that this was not his fight. None of it was. He had come back to the valley of the Jay intending to stay—only to find himself an outsider. The man who had raised him was dead; the girl who had said she would wait, had not waited.

Stevens crossed the street before he came abreast of the hotel. The slanting rays of the sun glinted from the badge on his black vest. His black hat rode far back on his head, covering thinning brown hair. He walked without hurry, his eyes on the road. But when he came abreast of the hotel Jerry saw the harsh lines around his mouth, the stiffness in his bony shoulders.

Jerry's lips tightened on his cigaret. He took a long last drag before discarding it. Then he found himself moving across the porch, down the stairs— heading across the street after the lawman.

Lafe Stevens stopped, turned a set face to Jerry's hail. He was frowning as Jerry walked to him. His regard dropped to the gun at Jerry's right hip, noting the way it was set. Slowly he eased the shotgun up across his waist.

"You got something on yore mind, Lannigan?" he asked bluntly.

Jerry shrugged. "I've been away a long time, Sheriff. I'm kinda curious about the other side of the river. Mind if I walk with you?"

The sheriff's gray eyes searched Jerry's face. Hope flickered up briefly in him. But his voice was stiff, unfriendly.

"I thought I had seen the last of you, when I heard you'd left the valley," he growled. "What brings you back?"

"Curiosity." Jerry's face had a quizzical smile. "I got twenty dollars riding on you, Sheriff. Mind if I come along?"

Stevens licked dry lips. He shook his head. "I don't mind, son," he said.

Jerry fell in step with him. Stevens paused at the bridge to shift the shotgun to his other arm. The narrow, dusty street at the other end of the plank span was empty—quiet in the fading sunlight. The Jay murmured sleepily below them.

Jerry loosened the Peacemaker in his holster. "Sundown always was peaceful, about this time," he murmured.

CHAPTER 5

The man watching from the doorway of the Lone Star Bar turned abruptly. "The sheriff's startin' across the bridge, Nate. Looks like he's gonna call you on Ellers—"

Nate Beals was sitting in a desultory game of poker. He tossed in his hand and walked heavily to the bar where a small, pock-faced man was idly wiping glasses. "Bourbon," he ordered harshly, and poured himself a drink from the bottle the barman slid on the counter.

The man who had been watching for the sheriff joined him. He was a long slab of a man with a dark, unsmiling face that gave no hint of his age.

A faint white scar broke the curve of his hawk nose.

The bartender slid him a clean glass, and he reached for the bottle of bourbon. He was Nate Beals' ramrod.

"There's someone with him," he added. "Doesn't look like his deppity."

Beals shrugged. "Didn't think the old fool would have the nerve." He took his drink like a man performing a distasteful task. He felt edgy. He knew his men were watching him, waiting for his orders.

Link Ellers, a slender, cold-faced man in his early twenties, sat by the rear wall. He had been dozing until Reo Cates' voice had awakened him. He pushed his hat back from straw-colored hair and licked his lips.

Beals reached for the bottle. In the bar mirror he saw himself, his broad, whiskey-flushed face marred by the long white scar that ran diagonally across his face, from his left temple to this jaw. There were other scars, but they did not show on Beals—they were branded in his soul.

Cates said: "He's carryin' a shotgun. Looks like

he means business." The ramrod had a soft voice, low, like a woman's.

Beals shrugged. "You know what to do," he growled. Cates smiled briefly. "Okay, boss." He moved away, joining the men at the poker table. One of them detached himself from the group and walked to the rear door and disappeared.

Beals brooded over his glass. Curse Ellers anyway! The man was a cold-blooded killer—he deserved to be hanged for the senseless killing of Charley. But he worked for the Lazy L. Inside himself Beals knew that if he hadn't stood by the man, the rest of his crew would have quit him. And he needed them in his fight against the H Bar H.

He met his burning eyes in the mirror, reflecting bitterly that he had changed greatly in the past year. The soft flesh of town living had been pared from him; he was still a heavy man, but his weight was solid on his frame. Wind and sun had marked his face, darkened and roughened it until there was small resemblance to the ruddy fullness of his mercantile store days.

Once he would have shrunk from seeing a man killed. Now he was going to stand by while a man he had called "friend" was shot down.

Slowly he lifted the glass to his lips. "*Prosit,*" he said softly, sneering at his reflection—at the scar that traced its way across his face and burned eternally in his soul.

Stevens paused at the foot of the saloon stairs, turning his attention to the cayuses nosing the long rail. The Lazy L was branded plainly on the nearest animal. He counted them slowly. "Eight of them," he said, and licked his lips.

Jerry said: "I think we can handle it." He said it matter-of-factly.

They went up the steps together, but the sheriff pushed his way inside first. He walked halfway to the bar before he stopped. Lannigan walked past him. The light was fading in the room—but he saw that Beals was standing alone at the bar. The others were clustered around the two rear card tables. There was no one else in the room.

Jerry saw this, and planned his move in the time

that it took him to reach the Lazy L owner's side. Beals had turned slowly as Jerry and the sheriff entered. Lannigan saw his eyes darken; little lines crinkled his forehead.

Then Jerry jammed the muzzle of his Colt into Beals' side!

It was a smooth, flicking motion that escaped the men clustered by the tables. They were watching the sheriff. Beals' involuntary gasp caught them by surprise.

"Which one, Sheriff?" Jerry said pleasantly.

Stevens swung the shotgun muzzles on Link Ellers. "I'll give you thirty seconds to get here," he ordered grimly.

Ellers glanced at Reo Cates for advice. The dark-faced ramrod shrugged. The killer's face twitched. This was not the way it had been planned. He got up, turning to Beals.

"He's got fifteen seconds," Jerry observed dryly. "If he makes a wrong move, you get the first slug," he told Beals.

Nate swallowed. "You heard the sheriff," he said. His voice was hoarse. "Get out there, Ellers!"

Link hesitated. Cates' soft voice purred: "Go ahead, Link. We'll get you out—later!"

The killer edged around a table and walked toward the sheriff, his boots scuffing softly over the scarred floor. Stevens' flat voice stopped him. "That's close enough! Now drop that gunbelt. *And be careful!*"

Link's fingers moved gingerly. He was looking into the twin muzzles of the 12 gauge shotgun, and from where he stood they couldn't miss. He loosened the buckle and felt his weighted holster drag his belt down.

"All right, Jerry," the sheriff said. "I think we've got—"

The bullet, hitting high up in the sheriff's back, knocked him forward. He fell on the shotgun, and one of the muzzles blasted a hole in the plank flooring.

Jerry jerked around with the roar of the Colt outside the batwings. He caught a glimpse of the back-shooter's boots under the batwings and he laced two shots, waist high, through the slatted wood.

The man outside the door gave a strangled, bubbly scream.

Link Ellers bent swiftly, reaching for his still holstered Colt. Jerry's snap shot broke his arm, just below the elbow. The killer stumbled, pain tearing a cry from his throat. He straightened, hugging his arm to his chest, his eyes glazed.

Beals hadn't moved—he hadn't had time to move!

Jerry's clipped voice stopped the men by the tables. "Tell them, Beals," he said thinly. "The first man who goes for a gun signs your death warrant!"

Beals flinched away from the hard muzzle in Jerry's fist. His voice was shaky. "You heard him!"

Reo Cates was standing spread-legged, a horny hand poised by his gun. He nodded slowly. "Reckon he's holdin' the top hand, boys," he muttered. His eyes were on the sheriff, who was making a slow, terribly determined effort to get to his feet.

Stevens' face was gray with pain. He pushed

himself up to his hands and knees and slowly dragged the shotgun toward him. The sweat on his face was visible across the room. He brought the gun up to his chest and swayed on his knees, his pain-filmed eyes surveying the room. Link Ellers edged away, moaning softly.

Jerry dug his gun into Beals' side. "You an' Ellers give the sheriff a hand!" he ordered grimly. "We're leaving together!"

Beals pushed away from the bar. But the sheriff got to his feet before they reached him. He cuddled the shotgun against his stomach, the muzzle menacing the men poised stiffly by the far wall.

"I'll walk out of here—Jerry," he said. "The way I came in!"

Jerry nodded. He grabbed Ellers by his shirt collar at the back of his neck. "Let's go!"

The sheriff backed out slowly, with Beals, Ellers and Jerry following. Beals stumbled over the body sprawled across the steps. His face was white and he looked sick.

They made a strange group heading back down that dusty road to the bridge. The sun was an orange stain behind horizon clouds.

The sheriff collapsed twenty yards from the bridge. He lay face down in the dust, a curiously crumpled, pathetic figure. Blood soaked the clothes that covered his back.

Jerry hesitated. Beals stood stolid, his scarred face a bitter mask. Ellers waited in tight-lipped silence.

The remainder of the Lazy L gunsters had crowded out to the Lone Star steps. They were bunched there, not more than two hundred yards away. Jerry swore thinly. A man with a rifle could change the entire picture.

Across the bridge a wagon was backing out into the dust of the street. The team of brown horses turned sharply, lunged into a sudden run. The wagon turned onto the bridge, the rumble of iron wheels and pounding hoofs booming heavily in the strained stillness.

Marion Akers pulled up by the sheriff. "Get him in the wagon," she said sharply. "Tommy'll watch them."

Jerry didn't waste time wondering what had

prompted the girl to come across the bridge. Tommy had swung the muzzle of his rifle to cover Beals.

Holstering his Colt, Jerry bent, got his arms under the unconscious lawman and dragged him up. Chest and shoulder muscles bulged with the effort. "Give me a hand here!" he snapped to Beals.

The Lazy L owner obeyed. They got Stevens' limp body into the wagon, wedged between several bags of grain and supplies from the general store. There was no room for anyone else.

Jerry stepped back, his Colt sliding into his fist again. "Get him to the doc, ma'am. I'll be along!"

The girl wheeled the team around in a tight circle and sent it lunging back across the bridge. Jerry caught a glimpse of her white face before she drove out of his line of sight. The memory of it remained with him—a picture of a resolute, courageous girl who had done on impulse what no one else in Sundown had thought of.

Beals turned a stubborn face to Jerry. "You got your man," he said thickly. "The law should be satisfied!"

Jerry said bleakly: "We'll walk across the bridge, together. The three of us!"

Beals cursed. Ellers looked at Jerry's gun and started walking.

On the other side of the Jay, Jerry paused. He could see the wagon drawn up before Doc Medill's office, two blocks down. Men were helping to get the sheriff out of the wagon.

"I reckon we can do without yore company," Jerry said flatly. He was looking at Beals' face, noting for the first time the extent of the whiplash scar across the man's features.

Beals licked dry lips. "You came back at the wrong time, Jerry," he whispered harshly. "I'm going to see that you regret this!"

Jerry smiled bleakly. "I wouldn't bet on it, Nate." He gave the man a hard shove. "You always liked the other side of the river—even in the old days. Liked to play around, after hours, with the *chiquitas*. A pretty fancy Dan—"

"I'll be back across the river, some day," Beals said grimly. "Don't forget it, Jerry—I'll be back!"

Jerry watched him go, his long, hard stride

sounding sharply in the twilight. Birds twittered sleepily in the thickets along the banks.

He turned to Ellers. "Let's go!" he said sharply.

Ma Jennings was in the room when Jerry entered. She was trimming the wick on a flower-glazed oil light on the stand by the bed. She was a heavy woman, a long-time widow, and she had developed a masculine directness about most things.

Lafe Stevens was in the iron-framed bed. The sheriff had been brought in from the doctor's office where Doc Medill had extracted the lead slug that had lodged under his shoulder. He moved restlessly, licking dry lips.

Jerry dropped his hat on a chair and moved to the bed. Ma Jennings fussed a moment with the bedding.

Lannigan said: "I got Ellers in a cell. The doc bandaged his arm." He pulled out a bunch of keys on a large key ring from his pocket and dropped them on the stand beside the bed. "You need a deputy, Lafe," he pointed out.

Stevens' gray eyes met his. Just below the sun-blackened line of his collar his skin was curiously white, speckled with brown spots.

"You did all right, son," the sheriff said. He spoke softly, as if it pained him. "The job's yours, if you want it."

Lannigan shook his head. "I'm leaving in the morning."

Stevens closed his eyes. Ma Jennings said softly: "He shouldn't talk so much, Jerry. The doctor said—"

"Leave us alone for a few minutes," Stevens said. His eyes were still closed. "I want to talk to Jerry, Ma."

The boarding house woman hesitated. "The doctor—"

"The devil with the doctor!" Stevens rasped. He looked at her, his eyes bright. "Leave us alone!"

Ma Jennings turned and went out.

Jerry frowned. Unconsciously he reached for his tobacco and papers, remembered the man on the bed had a bullet hole in him and started to put the fixings away. "Light up!" the sheriff growled. "This is goin' to take a few minutes to tell. You might as well be comfortable."

"You came back for some reason," Stevens said bluntly. "Was it Jed?"

Jerry took his time answering. His fingers, fashioning his cigaret, made their shadow pattern on the wall past the bed.

"No," he said quietly. "It wasn't Jed. I didn't know he had been killed until I got back."

Stevens made a short gesture with his hand. "I was going to write you. I kept track of you, off an' on. But I never thought you'd be back." He steadied his gaze on Jerry's eyes; they were bright in the yellow lamplight.

"Why did you come back, Jerry?"

Perhaps it was the intimacy of the scene in that quiet, lamp lit room, or the fact that Jerry himself had worn a marshal's badge for the past three years, that decided him. It might have been, too, that he had to tell someone—that the sharp and bitter disappointment he had suffered needed tell-ing.

"I came back to settle down, Lafe," he said. "I was tired of riding from town to town—tired of trouble. I came back to the valley of the Jay because this was the only home I had known." He smiled thinly. "All the time I was away I kept thinking of the valley—of Sundown. Whenever I ran into trouble, I remembered there was one place where a man could live in peace. I kept remembering Sundown in the evening—"

He took a long drag on his cigaret. Stevens was nodding slowly.

"I remembered a girl, too," he answered bitterly. "She said she'd wait." He leaned over and squashed the cigaret in a small bowl by the bed. "I came back to get married," he continued shortly. "But the girl didn't wait."

Stevens said slowly: "So you're hurt. There's trouble in the valley, an' it's spoiled the pretty picture you had made up in yore mind. Yore girl didn't wait—so you're done with us. Yo're gonna run away again—"

Jerry cut in sharply: "You forget I was a Crescent man, Stevens. No one was sorry to see me leave."

"Ah!" Stevens licked dry lips. "You never gave anyone a chance, son. You grew up with Jed, an' you got like him: suspicious, touchy. People take a man the way he wants them to, son—remember that. You were wild, and you were proddy about the Crescent. What did you expect?"

Jerry shrugged. "That was five years ago, Sheriff. Why should I stay now? I've got no stake in the valley."

The sheriff took a slow breath, wincing at the pain. "That's what I want to talk to you about," he said. "You have a stake. You own the Broken Circle."

Jerry frowned. "There's a man named Henry Akers—"

"I know," Stevens cut in tiredly. "He bought the place from the county. It was all legal. No one knew about the will Jed left—except me. I found it in his room, in a small tin box he kept in his dresser."

Jerry shook his head. "I don't want the place," he said. "Let the Akers keep it!"

"You wanted a reason to stay," Stevens growled. "You have it. Whether you want it or not, the Broken Circle is yores. An' the trouble that goes with it." His voice strengthened. "Someone bashed Jed's head in with a piece of cordwood, Jerry. Don't that mean anythin' to you?"

Jerry snapped testily: "What do you want me to do—take sides in this fight? Throw in with Houseman like he asked me? From what I heard about his trouble with Nate Beals, I'd say he asked for it. I don't blame Nate for hating Big Bill." He paced restlessly, angered by Stevens' blunt accusal. "Far as I can see it's a matter for Big Bill and Nate to settle—not mine!"

Stevens eased back like a man disappointed at not being understood. "A range war is always a bad thing, son," he said wearily. "A heck of a lot of innocent people usually get caught up in it before it's over. But if the only trouble was that between

Nate an' Big Bill, I'd feel less unhappy about it.

"I started workin' in the sheriff's office twenty years ago," he reminded Jerry. "I kind of grew up with the valley's troubles. Oh, there's been trouble, from time to time. But now it's gettin' way out of hand, Jerry. Both Nate and Big Bill have imported gunmen. And a lot of tough-looking jaspers have come in with them—they hang out across the river. They come and go as they please; they work for no one. I tell you, Jerry, the big trouble, when it comes, won't be between Beals and the H Bar H. When it breaks, both Houseman an' Beals will lose —they'll be stripped clean!"

He lay back, closing his eyes again to the sharp pain. His breathing was harsh. "You said you came home, Jerry," he muttered. "I'm glad you came back."

Ma Jennings came in, her face resolute. "You've had your five minutes," she said sharply. "You'll sleep now. I'm turning down the light."

Jerry turned to the door.

The sheriff's voice called painfully after him.

"You'll find a deputy's badge in my desk, Jerry. I'll be waitin' to swear you in."

Jerry didn't look back. He slammed the door as he went out.

CHAPTER 6

The Lazy L crew rode into the star-lit yard and pulled up before the ranchhouse. They had ridden back from town in sullen silence. Two horses trailed behind them—one riderless, the other carrying the dead man draped like a sack across the saddle.

Beals dismounted stiffly. "Bury it!" he ordered gruffly, and turned to the stairs. His heavy body cast a thick shadow momentarily against the door; then he opened it, slammed it shut behind him.

He stood in the dark, a big, stiff-backed figure, letting his anger ride him. Because of Ellers he had been forced into a stand he had not wanted, and his humiliation was greater because of it.

Beals had no illusions about his men. They worked for him because he paid them high wages; they stayed on because he had promised them a bonus when the showdown came with the H Bar H.

It was almost due. For more than six months he'd been laying his plans. Taking over, one by one, the worthless homesteads in the Crescent—ringing the H Bar H. When he was ready, when the time was ripe, he'd bring in the sheep—let them loose on H Bar H grass!

He sat in the dark, letting his thoughts take hold of him.

Out in the yard Reo Cates had wheeled his cayuse, put it to a walk to the bunkhouse. The others trailed after him.

The Lazy L ramrod dismounted and stood by the door. "Two of you get shovels," he ordered briefly. "Bury him behind the corral." He turned and went inside the bunkhouse and scraped a match. His hard face had a curious, undefinable smile. He found the light and turned up the wick. The shadows of the men crowding in behind flitted over the narrow bunkhouse walls.

Tony Argus, a squat, brown-skinned man with a nose spread across his face, said nasally: "What we gonna do about Ellers, Reo?"

Reo said indifferently: "We'll get him out when the time comes." He walked to the near bunk and sat down, his weight creaking the wooden frame. "We didn't do so badly," he said. "We scared the deppity out of the valley an' we laid up the sheriff. By the time he's up an' nosin' around again, it'll be over."

Tony spit on the floor. "We lost Kedder," he growled. "Link's in jail. I don't like it." He rubbed his palm over the butt of his gun. "Who's the hombre thet came in with the sheriff?"

Reo Cates shrugged. "Some high-minded citizen prob'bly," he sneered. "Forget him, Tony. If he butts in again, we'll take care of him."

He pushed his hat back on his head and got abruptly to his feet. "I'm headin' for the galley." He stopped in the doorway. "Be ready to ride in an hour," he ordered thinly. "We got a date with the boss—remember?"

An hour later he and Tony rode out of the Lazy L yard. They rode steadily, heading east until they topped the long, rock-strewn slope that formed a protective wall against the eroded country beyond. Below them the ranchhouse was a dark, shapeless blot; the light in the bunkhouse window was like a small, questioning eye in the night.

They turned north then, riding without conversation. A ragged half-moon lifted over the far hills, strengthening the starlight. Three hours of steady riding brought them to a small, rocky clearing. The land sloped away here, falling steadily to the bottomlands; the lights of Sundown shimmered in the rising ground heat, less than five miles away.

The "boss" was waiting for them. He was standing in the shadows, his back against a towering boulder. The red tip of a cigaret flared briefly.

Reo said softly: "You heard what happened in town?"

The man nodded. "You almost bungled it, Reo," he said. He had a hard, clipped tone. "I wanted the sheriff dead."

Reo said stubbornly: "I told Kedder to wait until the sheriff backed out with Link. The fool didn't wait!"

The man in the shadows made a curt gesture of dismissal. "Where's Davis and Whitey?" he asked sharply.

"Beals sent them out to the Homer place, in the Crescent," Cates said sullenly. "I told them to work over by the canyon pass an' make sure that the Akers place gets another goin' over."

"There was a craggy gent who sided in with the sheriff," Tony said bluntly. "He killed Kedder. You know who he was?"

The tall figure flicked his cigaret away in sudden anger. "Jerry Lannigan. He used to live here." There was a suppressed hatred in the man's voice that surprised Tony and Reo Cates.

"We'll make our move inside a week," he went on, controlling his voice. "I'll get word to you when to move."

"What about Beals?" demanded Cates. "Do we keep playing along with him?"

The other nodded. "We'll get rid of him before

we move. And Big Bill Houseman, too."

Reo Cates laughed softly. "Two darn fools!" he said succinctly.

"Don't get too cocky," the "boss" warned. "I'll see you here again next Friday."

Cates nodded. He and Tony were turning back to their horses when the tall man's voice added: "Just one more chore, Cates. I want you to get rid of Lannigan. I don't care how you do it—*but get rid of him!*"

Cates slid his hand down over the smooth handle of his Colt. "I'll see you Friday," he assented. "And Lannigan will be taken care of."

The same flattened moon shone through Jerry Lannigan's window, making a pale splotch on the worn throw rug. A soft warm breeze ruffled the sun-bleached lace curtains. The insect hum along the river came to the man on the bed, a peaceful full summer chorus.

Jerry Lannigan was stretched out, fully dressed, on the worn counterpane. He was very tired. Even his bones ached. But he was too restless to sleep. He swung his legs over the bedside and sat up, feeling in his pockets for his sack of tobacco. There was enough light coming through the window to fashion a cigaret; the sudden flare of his match as he lighted it limned his hard face.

He got up and walked to the window. His room fronted River Road. He looked down on the street, watching the late stage from Wilson swing down the street; the driver leaned forward over the dashboard. "Hi-ya!" the man growled, and the sound floated up to Jerry above the whirring wheels, the pounding hoofs.

Lannigan lifted his gaze across the river, to the long sweep of valley shimmering in the pale light. This was what he had come back for.

Stevens was right. He came to that conclusion, finally, as he looked out over the valley, not seeing, but sensing the long dark sweep of the Wall against the horizon.

Jed was dead—but in dying the man had given Lannigan a stake in the valley. The anchor he had been looking for. If he left now, Stevens would be right. Jed had understood, too. Five years ago he had run away—this time he would stay!

The breeze stirred the curtains slightly, ruffling them against his face. The moon and the night and the light touch against his cheek brought Gay sharply into his thoughts.

For the first time since he had left the H Bar H he faced the problem of this girl squarely. She hadn't waited. But she wasn't married yet. He had told her he'd come back. But it occurred to him with painful irony that when a girl said "forever" she meant only a reasonable time. Five years was a long time to wait, he admitted.

Sharply then, he felt the warmth of her kiss, the teasing regard of her eyes. Maybe, if he stayed, he'd still get what he had come back for.

He remained by the window a long time after making his decision, his thoughts drifting on, holding suddenly to Marion Akers' white, resolute face as she had wheeled the wagon back over the bridge. He had seen her and her brother briefly, in front of the doctor's office, just before they had headed out of town.

"I saw you needed help," she had replied to his

question. "The sheriff has been very friendly to us. I only did what I could."

He recalled this now, and it sobered him. It was going to be an unpleasant job to tell them they had to move. That the Broken Circle was his, and that he had decided to take over.

It still nagged at him when he finally turned in.

He waited until the sun had climbed to a respectable distance in the sky over Sundown the next morning before he dropped in on the sheriff. Ma Jennings cautioned him that the lawman had spent a restless night, to cut his visit short.

Stevens was awake when he entered. His face was drawn and gray in the morning light.

"I'll take that deputy's badge," Jerry said. He stood by the bed, looking down at the lawman. "Only until you get back on your feet, though. Then you get yourself another badgetoter, Lafe."

Stevens grinned faintly.

Jerry picked up the keys that still lay on the bedstand. "I'll be around later, when you feel stronger, so you can swear me in," he said. "Rest easy, Sheriff."

He walked down the street to the cubbyhole law office, let himself in with a key. There was an iron cot with a straw mattress by the wall, a rolltop desk with pigeonholes stuffed with papers, old letters and the miscellaneous accumulation of years, a dented brass cuspidor by the chair. A gun rack on the wall held three shotguns, two rifles. Both rifles were lever action Winchesters.

A rear door opened to a short, narrow corridor that ended in a blank wall. Two small cells flanked the corridor. Link Ellers was in the first one.

He sat up on his wall bunk when Jerry looked in on him. He looked dirty and tired, and blood had stained his arm bandage.

Jerry went back to the desk. A plain nickel badge with the simple word: *Deputy*, stamped across its face was in the middle drawer. He took it out, holding it in his palm. He wished suddenly that Jenkins had been here with him.

On the wall just past the cot there was a mirror. Sometimes Stevens shaved himself in his office.

Jerry Lannigan glanced into it as he pinned the badge to his shirt pocket. For the first time he noticed the spatter of freckles across the bridge of his nose, faint under the sun tan. He stepped back, and unconsciously dropped his right hand over the butt of his Colt.

Then he remembered that even a killer had to eat, and that it was the county's obligation to feed him while he remained in its custody.

He was conscious of the surprise his badge caused. Word will get around, he thought. It amused him. Jerry Lannigan, wearing a badge in Sundown!

He was crossing the street, coming back from the lunchroom with a tray for Ellers, when Gay Houseman hailed him. She was riding in a red-wheeled gig, sitting beside her brother, Dab, who was holding the reins of a matched team of high-spirited bays.

Jerry waited while the gig rolled toward him.

Gay Houseman was dressed comfortably. White blouse tucked into tan skirt, cream-colored Stetson, a yellow silk scarf, loosely knotted, giving color to the outfit. Beside her Dab Houseman hulked in dusty range clothes. He looked at Jerry with the dumb questioning of a mute animal.

"I thought you'd left," Gay said. She looked down at Lannigan as the gig stopped alongside him. "You were so angry yesterday—and so rude to poor Walter!"

The morning sun was on her face, bringing out the life and the sparkle in her wide gray eyes. The curve of her smooth throat brought the old pounding in Jerry's blood.

"I've decided to stay awhile," he said shortly. "And I'm sorry about poor Walter."

She laughed, a soft, tinkly sound. She turned to her brother. "Dab, I think I'll get out here. Wait for me at Mrs. Halloran's."

She swung her foot over the gig side and her heel caught on the round iron step protruding from the floor panel. She teetered precariously, gave a small, frightened scream, and threw out her arms as she fell.

Jerry dropped his tray and caught her. He felt her warm body against him, felt her move softly against his chest as he eased her down. Her hat had fallen from her head and her hair was in his face, yellow and soft as silk.

He steadied her on her feet, the blood pounding in his ears, shaking him with the intensity of sudden desire. She remained in his arms, her head tilting back, wide eyes suddenly teasing.

"Jerry," she whispered softly, "I really didn't think you'd come back."

He was conscious, then, that they were standing in the street—conscious, too, of Dab's dull face twisting animal-like as he came scrambling down from the gig. He released Gay abruptly.

Dab Houseman had a whip in his hand. He came at Jerry like a shambling bear, thick arm drawing back, lips curling away from yellowed teeth.

Jerry's right hand flicked downward, vanished behind a sudden burst of smoke. The whip in Dab Houseman's fist was sheared off neatly, leaving a stub three inches long.

The angry authority of that shot halted Dab and panicked the bays. They lunged away, pounding down the street, the gig bouncing behind them.

Gay whirled on her brother, her face furious.

"You thick-headed, dim-witted fool! I told you to wait for me at the Hallorans'! Now—" She stamped her foot, rage momentarily choking her.

Dab backed away like a cowed, confused dog.

"Go after that team," she ordered harshly. "If anything happens to them Paw'll have your hide!"

Dab turned and started lumbering down the street.

Jerry eased the gun back into his holster. He was looking at Gay, thinking that it had all been a little too pat, her tripping, falling into his arms. He was almost sure of it when a cold, intense voice behind him snapped: "You should have allowed Dab another try, Gay! Someone should give him a horse-whipping!"

Gay turned, brushing hair from her eyes. "Walter!" She seemed quite surprised. She made an attempt to straighten her blouse. "Really, Walter—" She laughed a little uncertainly. "It was an accident—"

The lawyer was on the boardwalk, about ten feet away. Jerry looked him over coldly.

"Maybe you think you're the man who can do

it?" he snapped.

The lawyer teetered on the edge of the walk, as though holding himself in. Neatly and quietly dressed as he was, there was a hardness about this man that challenged Jerry.

"Maybe some day I will!" he answered. He had control of himself now. He turned his attention to the girl beside Jerry.

"Gay! I want to talk to you!"

There was a possessiveness in his voice, a masculine certainty that tightened Jerry's lips.

Gay smiled teasingly. "I think I'd better leave," she said. "Walter's so jealous—" She waited for Jerry to pick up her hat. "Perhaps we can still meet—at the old rendezvous," she murmured.

Jerry watched her join the hard man on the walk, slip her arm under his. He was thinking that Gay had not changed at all. That the girl he had known at seventeen was still unsure of herself as a woman. And standing there, watching them go into Walter's office, Jerry had the premonition that Gay would never change—that the ready laughter, the teasing smile, the quicksilver moods he had found challenging in the past were part and parcel of Gay Houseman.

He became aware then that he was standing in the street, the spilled tray at his feet. Slowly he picked up the tray and headed back for the lunch-room.

CHAPTER 7

Jerry Lannigan, sheriff's deputy, left Sundown early next morning. He left the keys to the law office with Joe Semper and made arrangements for Joe to feed the prisoner.

"I don't think there'll be trouble," he told the saloon owner. "But I think I'll suggest to Stevens that we take Ellers to Wilson to stand trial. Some of those craggy Lazy L riders might take it into their heads to break him out."

He followed the Jay south for a few miles before turning west, striking across country for the Crescent. The sun was hot on his back. But there was a haze forming over Paler's Peak; by the time he had hit the rough country the haze had changed to thunderheads.

The freshness had gone out of the morning. There was a sultriness in the air, a stillness that forewarned of the gathering storm. Jerry had experienced the wild, slashing rains that sometimes whipped the valley, made impassable, swollen torrents of what had been dry gullies.

"Maybe we can make the Broken Circle before it breaks, Rebel," he muttered, and dug his heels into the roan's sides.

Three miles north two riders were jogging at a steady clip, heading for Homer's place. They had been up the better part of the night, and they rode in disgruntled silence.

The younger man's nose looked as though he had recently scoured it with a wire brush: it was scratched and swollen. He had difficulty breathing through it. He also favored his right hand; his wrist was stiff.

"I'm gettin' tired of this, Davis," he said thinly, breaking the morose silence. "What's come over the boss? If them nesters are in our way, why don't we ride in an' kick them out." He made a sound through his nose. "Tryin' to frighten them out by shootin' out their light at night ain't my idea—"

"Who asked for yore ideas, Whitey?" Davis growled. "Cates said we should scare the Akers out of the small valley. That's what we're doin'." He stopped to wipe his face with his dusty bandana. "It's hot," he complained sourly.

The thunderheads were reaching out across the valley, like a balled, dark blue fist. Lightning zagged a white streak of cosmic power earthward. The roll of thunder was still distant.

Davis looked behind him. They had been following a dry watercourse between low hills. "Let's get out of here," he snapped. "There's gonna be six feet of boilin' water comin' down here when that storm hits!"

They set their mounts to the nearer, rock-strewn slope. The thunder marched closer, like an artillery barrage lifting its firing range.

Whitey suddenly clutched Davis' arm. "Look!" he said. "Ain't that the hombre we ran into two days ago? The craggy jasper who said he didn't want trouble?"

Davis leaned forward, squinting. "Blamed if it ain't!" He scowled. "Wonder what he's doin', ridin' this way?"

Whitey edged his mount behind a boulder, drawing Davis with him. "I don't know what's he doin' up here," he muttered, "but I shore aim to find out." He touched his swollen nose, and his eyes glinted. "Looks like he's headed for the Akers place."

Davis suddenly swore. Something had caught his eye, a glint of metal on the rider's shirt. "A lawman! Must have been nosin' around Homer's place when we ran into him, Whitey." He turned and clamped his fingers over Whitey's arm as the man started to draw his rifle from his saddle boot. "Not now, you fool!" he snarled. "It's more'n five hundred yards, if it's an inch."

He cast a swift glance back the way they had come. "He's headed for the Akers place all right," he decided. "There's a place where—" He jerked his cayuse around. "Come on," he growled jubilantly. "I'll give you a good shot at that nosy badgetoter, Whitey. . . ."

Jerry stopped to rest his blowing roan. The sky was an ominous black over most of the valley; he could hear the rain in the distance. He turned a quick glance to the wagon road that skirted fifty-foot rock outcropping before angling up over a small hill. He was still three or four miles from the Broken Circle and he knew then that the storm would hit him before he made it.

He reached back to his cantle roll and fetched his slicker.

The big brindle dog came down the wagon road as Jerry swung the roan toward the Broken Circle. It had come padding out of the brush where it had been on some curious hunt of its own; now it stopped, ears pricking alertly. A low growl rumbled in his throat.

Jerry jerked the roan to a halt. The brindle was in the middle of the road, staring with some hidden knowledge of his own toward the rock outcropping. He turned his head, took a quick look at Jerry and uttered a soft, warning growl. . . .

Jerry lifted his frowning gaze to the cliff. The brindle evidently had been aware of his presence on the road before he showed himself to Jerry. From his behavior it was not Lannigan that was disturbing him; it had to be something further up the road.

"What is it, boy?" he asked softly. He was thinking back to the hot afternoon in Homer's deserted yard; remembering the beaten, bloody look in this animal's eyes as it had cowered back against the rope holding him; feeling again the icy tingling down his spine.

There was something wrong on the road! The brindle padded a few feet down the trail and stopped, its low growl breaking to a sharp, questioning bark.

Jerry swung abruptly out of saddle!

The bullet made a high, vicious whine overhead; the sharp rifle crack that followed was drowned in a sudden close burst of thunder. The rain came down in a scurrying patter of big drops, pelting Jerry's whirling body.

He jerked the rifle free of his saddle boot and slapped the roan's rump, sending the animal pounding away. The brindle had vanished into the brush with the rifle crack.

Two other shots cracked out, riding the trailing mutter of thunder. They followed each other so closely that Jerry, sprinting for the protection of the boulder off trail, guessed that they were two riflemen up on the outcropping.

Both shots came close. The first burned his side, tearing a jagged slash in his slicker; the second, taking the heel off his left boot, threw him off balance. He fell in a shallow dive and rolled desperately, cuddling his rifle to his body. Rain-spattered earth erupted two inches above his head; then he was up and tumbling behind the safety of the boulder.

He remained there, crouched, eyes bright with anger, only long enough to get rid of the binding slicker and catch his breath. The ambushers on the cliff, knowing they had missed, would also know they would be vulnerable to a flanking attack by the man they had hunted.

The rain came down, beating through the off-trail brush with wet, tearing sounds. In the interval between the first shot and his pause here behind the rock, visibility had been cut almost fifty percent. The world was suddenly a gray jumble of brush and rocks, lashed by sheets of rain that hissed through the underbrush, transformed every crack in the earth into a rivulet, every gully into a torrent.

Jerry slid away from the boulder. He was soaked to the skin before he had traveled ten yards.

He slid down into a pocket, splashed through several inches of water, and scrambled up the other slope. The old intimate feel of this country came back to him as he circled through the brush for the timbered spine of the outcropping.

Lightning split the grayness with a vividness that hurt his eyes. The report followed on the heels of the white flash, a flat abrupt sound that shook the earth. Jerry wiped the rain from his eyes.

He crouched and wiped his eyes again, not believing his luck!

Ahead of him, huddled against the partial protection of a rock, were two horses! They shifted nervously, jerking their heads up, fighting their reins which were looped around the branches of a scrub oak. Jerry could see their eyes roll with each jagged flash of lightning and subsequent roll of thunder.

"Beat them," he whispered grimly, and shifted his grip on the wet rifle. He was moving forward into the small clearing when the two men broke through the wet brush.

They didn't see him. Jerry recognized them— the two Lazy L riders he had run into at Homer's old place.

Whitey was jerking the reins of his horse loose, twisting up into saddle, when Jerry yelled: "Over here, Lazy L!"

Davis whirled. Like Jerry, he was hugging his rifle to him. He saw Lannigan's rain-blurred form across the small clearing and he dropped his rifle, deciding, in that split second, that he could do better with his Colt. His fingers tightened on the wet handle; he jerked it clear before Jerry's slug passed through his body.

Whitey cast a startled look over his shoulder as he wheeled his mount. Jerry was running toward him. The thin-faced gunster flattened over the horn, raking his spurs deep into the cayuse's flanks.

Jerry slammed a shot at the looming bulk and tried to twist away from that plunging animal. He slipped on muddy underfooting, and then the horse's wet shoulder slammed him aside. He lost the rifle as he went down in a muddy sprawl. The Lazy L animal plunged past, started up the small slope beyond the clearing and lost its footing.

Jerry was on his hands and knees, searching for the rifle, when he saw the animal topped backward. Whitey was flung out of saddle like a rag doll. His head hit a rain-slicked boulder with a sodden thunk; then the horse fell on him.

The animal's wild scream was lost in a heavy burst of thunder!

Lannigan crawled to his feet. The animal was threshing around at the bottom of the slope. Slowly Jerry walked to it, the rain driving against his back. When he was three feet away he levelled the rifle and put a bullet through the horse's head.

The beating rain chilled him. While he had been moving, tensed for trouble, his body had shed the discomfort of his soaked clothes. Now, as he straightened wearily, he felt stiff and uncomfortable.

He turned and started back for the wagon road. It was going to be a long four miles to the shelter of the Broken Circle. . . .

From where she sat, on the porch of the ranchhouse, Marion Akers could see the storm clouds piling up over the lower valley. She had been sitting there beside her mother, a thin, pallid-faced woman with bright blue eyes, for more than an hour. The woman had been reading from a small black-bound book—but she had stopped when her daughter's attention had wandered. She watched Marion for a while; then she sighed. "I'm afraid 'The Shropshire Lad' has little interest for you today, my dear."

Marion turned and put a hand on the woman's pale arm. "I'm sorry, Mother." She made a little face, her eyes crinkling. "But the country here is so beautiful—"

Elizabeth Akers nodded gently. "I like it here, Marion. If only—"

She let her gaze move on to where Henry Akers, bent and tired, was standing by the smoldering ruins of the small shed that had housed their two milk cows. He looked old and defeated, running long fingers nervously through his thin gray hair.

Marion's lips tightened. Why didn't they leave them alone?

They had bothered no one, they asked little of anyone. They had taken no sides in the trouble in the valley. Yet persistently they had been plagued by trouble. Fences torn down, chickens wantonly killed, shots through the windows. And now, last night, the small barn had been set afire; only Tommy's alertness had saved the milk cows.

As if her mother had sensed her thoughts, she asked: "Where's Tommy? I haven't seen him since morning."

Marion shrugged. "He went off with Buddy."

The small figure appeared briefly among the scrub oak across the Upper Jay, then appeared clearly as he struck out across the small meadow toward the ranchhouse. Marion said: "He's coming home now, Mother."

Henry Akers intercepted the boy, and they came on to the house together. Henry cast a worried glance at the piling clouds. The wind freshened, made sounds in the tall pines behind the house. The pages ruffled in Elizabeth Akers' hands.

She shivered a little. "It is going to storm," she said sadly. She started to raise herself from her chair, and her husband slipped his arm under her shoulders. "Liz," he said, "I've had enough. I want to take you back. Perhaps in St. Louis—"

Elizabeth Akers shook her head. "I'm going to die here, Henry," she whispered. "It's clean and big—and restful. Yes, even with the trouble we've been having. They want us to leave, whoever it is. But, Henry," she lowered her voice, "I don't feel I could stand to move again. I don't want to, Henry!"

He did not persist. They went on into the house. But Marion remained on the porch. Tommy turned to stare down the small valley.

"Where's Buddy?" Marion asked.

"Out there." Tommy made a brief gesture. He was a serious boy for his years. He had never been a talkative youngster, and in the past months he had grown quiet, answering mostly in monosyllables.

But he turned to her now, bright excitement in his eyes. "Sis, I saw them. The two men. I followed their tracks this morning, Buddy and I. There's a crack in the Wall, just over that ridge. A narrow passageway. When they had gone, I went down. It leads back into the Wall for a long way. I don't know how far, but I bet it goes all the way through."

Marion frowned. It had been a long speech for Tommy. Now, looking at him, she caught some of his excitement.

"They were the ones who burned our barn," Tommy said. "One was pretty old, almost as old as Paw. The other was younger, but he had white hair. I saw it when he took off his hat to scratch his head. I know it was them," he added swiftly. "I followed their tracks from the barn."

"Did you tell Dad?"

Tommy's face grew sullen. He shook his head. "You know Paw doesn't want me to leave the valley." He turned as the faint mutter of thunder rolled along the horizon. "I wish Buddy'd get back."

Marion said: "He'll show up, Tommy. Better go in. I think Dad'll need you. I hear him trying to board up the window they broke last night."

Tommy turned reluctantly to the door.

Marion waited. The piling clouds, racing swiftly toward her, gripped her with their terrible majesty. Even as she waited the first dark mass thrust overhead, and the spatter of rain was almost simultaneous. A few big drops plopped into the dusty yard, heralding the deluge to come.

Lightning tore its zigzag path over the far ridge, and now the roll of thunder bounced back from the Wall, magnifying the sound, prolonging the heavy mutter.

Reluctantly Marion followed her brother into the house. . . .

The violence of the storm passed, thunder was a low growl in the distance, when Marion heard boots grate heavily on the steps. Fear knifed through her. She turned to where her father was sitting with Tommy before the fire flickering in the stone fireplace, and she saw her fear reflected in his thin face.

Tommy reached for the rifle that stood in a corner. Henry Akers did not stop him.

The man stood outside in the steady rain and knocked on the door. No one moved inside the house. Henry Akers swallowed.

Tommy started for the door. But Marion moved between him. Her fingers closed over the latch. The man pounded on the door again.

Marion jerked it open. Behind her Tommy stood spread-legged, his rifle held ready.

The man on the porch was hatless, his hair plastered on his head. His shirt clung to his thick chest. He looked as though he had come a long way in this rain and had either fallen or rolled in the mud. His pants were torn above the knees and his face was scratched. He was holding a rifle in his left hand; Marion saw the butt of a Colt in his holster.

Slowly the man lowered his rifle to the porch, propping it against the side of the house. "The fire looks good, miss," he said tiredly. "May I come in?"

Marion's eyes rested briefly on the badge pinned to this man's shirt, raised again to the strong, blunt-chinned face. This was the man who had ridden across the Upper Jay two days before, asking about Jed Lafreau. The same man, she remembered, who had gone with Sheriff Stevens across the river. . . .

He moved his wet shoulders in a stiff, impatient gesture. "I'm harmless, Miss Akers," he said wearily. He took his Colt out of holster and held it out to her, butt first. "May I come in?" he repeated stubbornly.

Marion took the heavy Colt and stepped aside. Jerry grinned coldly. He walked past her to the fire, stopping beside Henry Akers, and stretched his wet hands out to the blaze.

"I grew up here," he said. "This is the first time I've been back in five years." He turned his back to the fire, his eyes going back across that room, meeting Marion Akers' wide eyes. "Name's Jerry

Lannigan. I was raised by Jed Lafreau."

The rain swept dismally across the yard; Jerry could see, through the open door, the Upper Jay fretting against its banks. For an exasperating moment he felt like a man who had been talking to people who couldn't hear him, for no one had moved.

Then Marion Akers closed the door and came across the room to him. "Dad!" she said quietly. "I think he can get into some of your old clothes. I'll get coffee on the fire."

Henry roused himself. "Of course, of course." He turned to Jerry. "My wife's asleep. If you'll come into my son's bedroom—"

Jerry nodded. He stopped by Tommy, his voice grave. "Had a rifle like that myself, when I was your age." He reached out and took it from the boy's hands. Tommy jerked. Jerry looked it over, smiled as he handed it back. "It'll shoot better with a new firing pin," he said, and followed Henry into the bedroom. . . .

Tommy scowled. But Marion stood a moment, staring toward the door of Tommy's room. For

the first time in her life she had become aware of
a man—and the impact of the realization shook
her, sent the blood into her cheeks. She turned
swiftly to the kitchen, not wanting Tommy to
see. . . .

CHAPTER 8

The storm had let up earlier in Sundown. By dark the rain had slackened, fallen to a thin drizzle. Patches of starry sky showed through breaks in the cloud mass.

Sundown glistened in the rain, wet buildings reflecting the yellow glare of lamps. Drain spouts still dribbled water into barrels already overflowing. River Road was fetlock deep in mud; the puddles reflected the glare from saloon and store windows.

The Jay ran swollen, its water lapping the underside of the sturdy plank bridge.

Joe Semper belched softly. He glanced at the clock on the shelf behind him and suddenly remembered he had not fed Link Ellers since morning. For a moment he was tempted to let it go until tomorrow morning. The man Ellers had killed had been a friend of Joe's; he had little liking for the job Jerry Lannigan had entrusted him with.

Earnie, his night relief, had come in and was washing glasses behind the bar. Joe moved over to him. "I'm goin' out for a half-hour," he said. He picked up the law office keys and thrust them into his pocket.

Earnie, a red-faced, balding man nodded. He looked out over the small crowd. "Why don't you go home?" he suggested. "With this rain it looks like a slow night."

Joe shrugged. "Yeah—I think I will." He took off his apron and hung it on a hook. "Good night, Earnie."

He paused on the walk outside the bar and took a breath of the clean, wet night. Jerry Lannigan had not returned, and he let his thoughts move along this pattern as he headed for the lunchroom. A wild kid, he mused; even then Jerry had been a dangerous man with a gun. Or with fists. More than one man in Sundown, hearing that Jerry had left the valley, had prophesied he'd turn outlaw. It had surprised everyone when news dribbled back that Jerry Lannigan was making a name for himself as town marshal.

Now he had come back, and it suddenly struck Joe Semper as ironical that Jerry Lannigan was the man Sundown needed.

He pushed open the door of the lunchroom and slid a leg over an empty stool, settling his frame wearily on the seat. "Supper menu," he told the man behind the counter. "On a tray."

The counterman yelled his order through an opening in the rear wall. Then he turned and leaned his elbows on the wood. It was past the rush hour and time hung a little heavy.

"If I had anything to do with it," he said belligerently, "I'd wrap a rope around his neck, instead of feeding him!" He stared at Joe, hoping for an argument, but the barman shrugged.

"Can't see wasting good food on a skunk like that," the counterman persisted. "Comes out of the taxpayers' pockets, too." He didn't pay any taxes, but he did not let this interfere with the fervor of his indignation.

Joe was tired. The old pain gnawed at his stomach. He wished he could smoke, but experience told him he would suffer more than it was worth. He slapped his palm on the counter, and the man behind it opened his mouth, getting ready to shred any comment Joe was about to make.

"Gimme a glass of milk," Joe said.

The counterman's mouth remained open. It stayed open so long Joe grew alarmed. "Milk," he said. "You know—it comes from cows."

The counterman clicked his teeth. Wordlessly he served Joe his milk, and as silently, a few minutes later, placed the tray in front of the weary bartender.

Joe paid him, picked up the tray, and went out.

He walked down the walk, his feet making a shuffling, dragging sound. He passed by Attorney Walter K. Burke's office, and noticed that the lawyer was working late tonight.

He let himself into the dark office, placed the loaded tray on the desk, and fumbled for a match.

The air was close in the small room. He found the lamp, and a moment later the yellow glow reached out across the floor to the walls.

Joe left the keys on the desk.

He opened the door to the cells, then went back and picked up the tray and the lamp. Looking through the iron grill, he saw that Ellers was lying on the cot.

He said loudly: "Hey!"

Link stirred. He sat up and ran the fingers of his left hand through his hair. He needed a shave, and he looked dirty.

Joe growled: "I brought you something to eat." He placed the lamp down in the small corridor and started to slide the tray under the iron door. Link watched him without moving.

Joe straightened. "I'll be back for the tray in the morning," he said. He heard a step behind him and turned quickly. "Oh!" he said, relieved. "I thought it was—"

Jammed just under his heart, the .38 made surprisingly little noise. Joe seemed to rise up on his toes, his mouth opening, trying to suck in air. His blue eyes had a startled look in them.

His killer caught him as he fell, dragged him swiftly to one side. A key grated in the lock, the cell door swung open.

A hard voice said sharply: "There's a leggy sorrel waiting for you at the rail, two doors north. Walk slow, and keep to the shadows."

Ellers nodded. He stepped through the door and went into the office. The man who had freed him waited. Ellers' boots tapped softly on the walk, heading north.

Then the killer picked up the lamp and walked back to the office. He left Joe lying in the corridor, closing the door on the body. He put the lamp on the desk, and dropped the keys beside it.

He chuckled coldly a second before he blew out the light. Then he turned and walked out of the law office, closing the door softly behind him.

Jerry left the Akers' early next morning. Sometime during the night the roan had wandered in, reins dragging. Tommy had found him when he heard Buddy bark, around daybreak, and went out. The roan was standing with drooping head by the corral. Its saddle had slipped down under its belly—

With Tommy watching, Jerry had given the roan a rubdown, draped a worn but dry blanket over its back, and measured out oats in the bucket.

The unfriendliness had gone out of Tommy's face. He sat cross-legged, listening to Jerry tell of his boyhood here. . . .

Watching her brother from the window, Marion thought with a sharp pang of realization, that Tommy needed the company of men—at least the company of a man not too far removed from him in years. Her father had married late; he was more than forty years older than Tommy. And he was not himself; he was worried about Elizabeth, and he was out of his environment here. . . .

Behind her, in the kitchen, she heard her mother singing. Elizabeth had not seemed so happy in years. Even her father's voice seemed gay.

Was it because of Jerry? Did they feel, as she did, the quiet strength in this man, the sureness of his actions—a feeling that was so badly needed here?

They had drawn him out last night, sitting around the fire. Wearing Henry's clothes, he seemed to fill them out, straining the gray wool shirt he had not been able to button at the throat.

He had told them about his life here, about Jed; he had grown laconic, however, when he spoke of the five years he had been away. And he had skimmed over what had happened in town.

"The sheriff needed help," he said simply. "I went along, like any good citizen." He shrugged. "I promised Stevens I'd wear his deputy's badge until he got well enough to take over again."

But watching him, Marion had sensed the violence in this man, and it had repelled and fascinated her. When Tommy had mentioned the two men he had seen on Broken Circle ground and asked Jerry if he had seen them, too, Lannigan had nodded. But he had ventured no further comment.

Several times, while talking about Jed, Lannigan had seemed about to say something further; then he had looked at Elizabeth Akers, as if her mother held some peculiar meaning for him.

"You like it here, Mrs. Akers?" he had asked gently.

Marion remembered her mother's answer, and the look that had briefly clouded Jerry's face.

Outside, Jerry had mounted the roan. He turned and rode toward the steps, and Marion went to the door. Lannigan said quietly: "I've never spent a better evening, Marion."

Her father and mother came to the door with her. Henry's voice held a new assurance. "Come back any time, Jerry. We want you to feel this is your home, as much as ours."

Jerry smiled. "I do," he said politely. He reached down and ran his fingers over Tommy's hair. "Take care of them, Tommy," he said. He waved to the figures in the doorway.

The roan, glad to work the chill from its bones, stretched out as he headed down the wagon road to town.

CHAPTER 9

A crowd was collected about the law office when Jerry rode into Sundown. He nosed the roan in at the nearest rack and pushed his way through the curious onlookers into the office.

Doctor Medill, a short, wizened man with snapping black eyes, was talking to a red-faced man Jerry recognized as working for Joe Semper. The doc's voice was devoid of emotion. "He's been dead since early last night, Earnie. He needs an undertaker—"

He turned as Jerry came in. He and Earnie saw the badge on Jerry's shirt, and both men frowned.

Jerry said sharply: "What's wrong, Doc?"

Medill waved a careless hand toward the bunk.

Jerry turned. Joe Semper lay on the thin straw mattress. He was dead.

Earnie said harshly: "Ellers is gone. Someone killed Joe last night an' let the killer out!"

Jerry bent by Joe's body. He could see the powder burns around the bullet hole just under the dead man's left breast. Joe had not bled a lot.

The doc said professionally: "Bullet ranged upward, possibly tearing through left ventricle. Whoever shot him held the muzzle against his chest."

Jerry straightened. He was thinking that whoever had killed Joe must have been someone the bartender knew, knew well enough not to suspect danger from that quarter. Yet who, other than the hardcases working for the Lazy L, would want Link Ellers free? And Joe Semper would never have allowed one of Beals' gunsters to get that close. . . .

Earnie said angrily: "I should have checked earlier, Jerry. But I knew Joe wasn't feelin' too good when he left last night to look in on Ellers; he said he was goin' home right after." He swore feelingly. "I was havin' a late breakfast at the lunchroom when Sam came in and asked me if I had seen Joe. The counterman remembered Joe had not brought back his tray, so I came over here to check. The door was unlocked. The keys"—he pointed to them, lying on the desk by the lamp— "were right there. When I opened the door to the cells, I saw Joe. The cell door was open; Link Ellers was gone. I dragged Joe in here and got him on the cot. I knew he was dead, but I went and got the doc anyway."

Medill picked up his black bag. "I'll send McIntosh over for the body; it's his job now," he said. He pushed his way out through the crowd.

Jerry dispersed the crowd. Earnie waited until the undertaker came for the body; then he left with it.

Lannigan stood in the doorway, looking down the muddy street. There was a clean fresh smell in the air, still damp from last night's rain. The Jay still ran muddy and swollen between its banks.

He had taken on the job as deputy without any formulated conception of what he was up against. He was still thinking of Sundown as he remembered it—drowsy and peaceful under the summer sun.

But now, as he stood there, a hardness ridging his blunt jaw, he examined the pieces, one by one. Jed had been killed, clubbed to death. When the Akers took over Jed's place, someone began what could only be a systematic campaign to drive them out. Were the two incidents connected? Was the Broken Circle important enough to someone to want the Akers driven off? Why? What was there up at the small ranch that anyone would want badly enough to kill for it?

He remembered that Davis and Whitey had taken over the Homer place for Nate Beals. If there was little enough value to the Broken Circle, there was none at all to the old Homer place.

Both Beals and Houseman had imported gunmen; both ranches were now armed camps, each waiting for the other to make a wrong move. But was this the real danger in the valley?

Jerry frowned. The closer he examined what he knew, the more he suspected there was something bigger than a threatening range war to contend with. Beals' Lazy L gunsters had maneuvered the sheriff into a trap across the river; if things had gone the way they planned, Stevens would have been killed and Ellers probably left the valley. The killing would naturally have been laid to Link, who would be long gone by the time anyone else picked up the sheriff's star. And in that interval the valley would be without any law enforcement.

Only the fact that he had gone with Stevens had disrupted their plans, nor had they expected him to wear a deputy's badge.

Jerry grinned bleakly. At the moment he was the only law in the valley and he knew what that meant.

He had been ambushed yesterday—they would try again!

He remembered then that, though he had a star on his shirt, he was still without legal authority. He had to see Sheriff Stevens, get sworn in. . . .

Stevens was propped up with pillows, sipping at a clear soup, when Jerry walked in on him. Pinpoints of gray beard roughened the old lawman's jaw.

Jerry said: "I won't take long, Sheriff." He took the soup from the lawman and placed it on the night stand.

Ma Jennings came in and started to say something. Jerry took her gently by the shoulders and turned her toward the door. "I'll see that he gets his soup, Ma," he said sharply. "And his rest, too."

He closed the door behind her and turned to the bed. Stevens was grinning. "You shore have a way with wimmen, Jerry," he said. "She's been fussin' over me like a cluckin' hen since I got hurt." But Jerry could see that the old bachelor liked it.

"You heard about Joe gettin' killed and Link Ellers getting busted out," he asked grimly.

The sheriff nodded. "Ma told me, when she brung in the soup." He listened as Jerry explained what had happened out in the Crescent.

Stevens brushed his hand across his mustache. "You tell the Akers to move out, Jerry?" His blue eyes had a clear innocence.

Jerry frowned. "I figger that's your job, Sheriff," he growled. "You were responsible for letting them buy Jed's place without a clear title."

Stevens snorted softly. The gesture drew a wince of pain across his face.

Jerry unpinned his badge, laid it on the bedstand. "I want this job made legal, Sheriff," he growled. "But before you swear me in I want to have things clear. When I pin on that badge I want to have a free hand. I'll handle the law end my way, until you get on your feet. I want that understood, Stevens."

The lawman looked up into Jerry's hard face. "I'll take a chance on it," he said simply.

He swore Jerry in, and watched the other pin the badge over his shirt pocket. "What you gonna do now?" he asked.

Jerry said: "First I'm going to send a wire to a friend of mine in Wyoming. Then I'm riding up to see Nate Beals."

He thrust the soup bowl into Stevens' hands before the other could comment. "I promised Ma you'd have your soup and rest," he grinned. "Don't make a liar out of me."

He closed the door on Stevens' spluttering. . . .

The stage office clerk took the note Jerry handed him, read the brief message. He nodded. "I'll have George drop this by the telegraph office in Wilson when he comes through."

Jerry said: "Ask him to look for an answer on his way back." He turned away, feeling a faint satisfaction ease the tension in him.

He didn't see the lawyer until the man's sharp voice cut across his thoughts. "You work pretty fast, Lannigan." There was a sneer attached to the hard voice. "For a saddle bum who just drifted back into the valley!"

Jerry turned around. There was more than dislike in this man's voice; there was a cold and implacable hatred that crawled through Lannigan, shocked him into grim alertness.

The lawyer had a leather grip in his hand and he was dressed for travelling. He had evidently come across the street, for he was just now stepping up to the boardwalk a few paces from the deputy.

He stopped and dropped his bag, a tall, hard-bodied man dressed almost nattily in town clothes. The heavy watch chain looped across his gray vest caught the sun and glittered with yellow brilliance. At the bottom of the loop a miniature silver Colt dangled.

"Stevens must have gone soft in the head," the man continued contemptuously, "when he deputized you. From what I've heard about you, Lannigan, I'm not surprised that a killer like Link Ellers broke jail last night."

Several men had stopped, listening, on the walk. Several others came to nearby doors, attracted by the lawyer's sharp voice.

This was the man Gay Houseman was marrying, Jerry thought bleakly. It could be that jealousy was riding this man; Gay had deliberately played up to him, he remembered grimly, the day she had come to town. But somehow Jerry sensed something more than jealousy in this man's tone, in his deliberate challenge.

He started to turn away, not wanting to get into this trouble, not wishing to give Gay the perverse satisfaction of knowing he and her fiancé had fought.

"I knew you were yellow, too," the man sneered.

Jerry turned. He closed the distance to the man in three long strides. The lawyer's hands came up a little late to block Jerry's palm. The slap was like a rifle crack in the morning stillness.

Walter's head jerked. For an instant his right hand dropped, slid futilely over his gunless thigh; it was an instinctive gesture that quickened Jerry. Then the man lunged for the deputy, jabbing a straight left into Jerry's mouth.

Blood tasted salty on Jerry's tongue. He fell back, blocking Walter's right with his shoulder. Those were the only two punches the lawyer landed.

Jerry moved in under another left and buried his fist in the man's unprotected stomach. The attorney's whooshing grunt was heard for half a block. He seemed to come apart; his raised arms faltered, his knees buckled. His hard, dark face sagged, turned a muddy coffee color.

Jerry's right hand jerked his head around. He was falling when Jerry hit him again, a savage blow that dropped the man across the stage office doorway.

Jerry stood over the unconscious man, violence still shading his eyes. Slowly he wiped the blood from his split lips.

Turning then, he strode across the walk to the roan waiting patiently at the rack.

CHAPTER 10

Big Bill Houseman stood in his stirrups, his scowling gaze reaching across the backs of the milling steers. He had been riding since morning, and the shirt was plastered across his broad back. He had always outworked any two men he had ever hired, and he had done it again these past days.

But the thought held little satisfaction for him now. He had not seen either Dab or Bob in the past hour, and anger swept over him, tightening the thin line of his lips.

"If either of them dared to quit on me—" he growled. He edged his tired cayuse around the herd, looking for his sons, and finally swung away with a curse. He had ridden both of them unmercifully. They were his sons, and because of this he made them toe a mark of killing work in front of these hard-eyed, sweating men he had hired.

Rod Harrison, his foreman, was bent over the water pail by the chuckwagon. He turned as Big Bill rode up, holding a dipper in his hand.

"Saw them ride off just as I came down thet draw with a couple of two-year-olds," Harrison drawled an answer to Big Bill's barked question. "They were headed for the ranch, I reckon."

Big Bill's face darkened. He slid stiff-legged out of saddle. "I'll show 'em!" he grated thickly. "I'll drag them both back by the scruff of their necks—" He whirled to the horse wrangler standing by the wagon. "Get me a fresh cayuse! The big sorrel! Darn it, yuh bandy-legged jackass—*move!*"

The wrangler, a slim, tow-haired man, eased away from the wagon. Harrison straightened, his shoulder muscles stiffening. He had been with Big Bill for ten years and he had an unswerving loyalty to his boss.

The wrangler spat slowly into the dust. Then he turned and walked off toward the remuda, limping slightly from an old break in his right leg.

Big Bill sighed, his temper settling. He walked to the water bucket, took the dipper from Harrison's hand and thrust it into the water. He drank noisily, gustily.

"Keep 'em workin'!" he growled to his foreman. "I want to be ready to drive in the mornin':"

The H Bar H ramrod nodded. "There's close to fifteen hundred head out there now," he muttered. His eyes glinted with thin satisfaction. "All prime beef."

Big Bill nodded. "I'll feel better when we get 'em loaded into cars at Wilson," he growled. He let his scowling gaze range northward, where low hills shut off the horizon. Nate Beals' Lazy L lay off in that direction.

Harrison followed his gaze and understood the bigger man's worry. He said thoughtfully: "He's bound to make his move soon, Bill. That craggy guncrew he's payin' wages to must be gettin' restless. There ain't enough work on Nate's two bit spread to work a third of the men he's hired."

Big Bill sneered. "Let him make a move, Rod! Just one excuse, I want! We'll ride down on that mangy spread of his an' wipe him out! I'll make that white-livered dry goods clerk sorry he ever threatened the H Bar H."

He flicked the water dregs from the dipper as the wrangler came up, leading the big sorrel. The slim man snubbed the high-spirited animal to the wagon wheel and started to strip Big Bill's saddle from the drooping-headed bay.

The H Bar H boss watched him in moody silence. The edge of his anger had dulled; he had no rancor for the man.

The wrangler finished transferring the saddle to the sorrel. He stepped back and watched Big Bill climb stiffly into saddle, jerk the animal's head around. The sorrel whirled, started off at a run.

"Hope he breaks his neck," the wrangler said through his teeth. He turned and caught Harrison's scowling stare. The wrangler spat on the ground and walked away. . . .

It was past noon when Big Bill thundered into the H Bar H ranchyard. Bob Houseman was sitting on the porch. He didn't move when he saw his father. He had washed the dust and grime from his thin face and changed clothes. His lips tightened as Big Bill rode into the yard, up to the stairs, and dismounted. The blowing sorrel snorted and wandered off toward the corral.

Big Bill's fists were clenched as he started up the stairs. "Where's Dab?" he asked harshly.

Bob rose slowly. "I don't know," he said.

"Blast you!" his father bellowed. "Don't lie! Harrison saw yuh ride off together!"

Bob's lips whitened. "I don't know where Dab is," he repeated stubbornly. "He just left me—rode off toward the creek." He dropped his gaze from his father's face. "You know Dab," he muttered. "When he gets a mind to something—"

"I know Dab!" his father snarled. "I know you, too! You put him up to it! He wouldn't have quit, if yuh hadn't put it in his head—"

"We had enough!" Bob interjected, white-lipped. "Maybe you can drive yore men like animals, those who don't quit first! But I've had enough! You've ridden us both since Mother died! I've taken it, because I've been afraid of you!" There were tears in Bob's eyes now, tears of rage, of impotent frustration.

"I've always been afraid of you! So has Dab. He's big, he's strong—like you. Only he's slow upstairs—he's dumb, like an ox!" Bob's voice shook with feeling. "That's what you always told him. He's dumb, he thinks you're God—but he's afraid of you! That's why he didn't come home with me! He got afraid—"

Big Bill was standing, frozen. A big man, made of granite, of unyielding stone.

"Yuh yeller-backed cur!" he rumbled. "You no-good, snivelin'—" He took two steps forward and cuffed Bob across the face.

The smaller man spun around, fell across the veranda railing. He hung jackknifed for a moment, breathing raggedly. Then he straightened. He pushed away with both hands, and when he faced his father his Colt was in his fist. He held it levelled at the big man's stomach, and the hate in his son's eyes, more than the threat of that muzzle, made Big Bill flinch.

In that moment Death hung by a thread. Slowly, with terrible deliberation that brought the sweat out over Bob's blazing eyes, he caught hold of himself.

His lips twisted with a cold and terrible satisfaction at the look in his father's eyes. "I could have killed you!" he whispered harshly. "I could have killed you—but I let you live! I want you to remember that!"

He jammed the gun down into his holster and pushed past his father, standing stonelike by the railing. He walked down the stairs with a swagger that was new to him.

Big Bill roused himself as Bob caught the sorrel's trailing reins and swung into saddle. He came to the stairs, moving like a man in a trance.

"Bob!" he called. His voice was strained, caught somewhere in his throat. "Bob—where're you goin'?"

Bob leaned forward over the horn. The transformation in him shook Big Bill. "Anywhere," Bob said flatly. "Anywhere, so long as it's a whale of a long way from here!"

He jerked the sorrel's head around, his back stiff and proud with a newfound self respect.

Big Bill took one faltering step after him. But the naked hate he had seen in his son's eyes was like a knife, twisting deep in his bowels, draining him of resolution.

He turned, dragging his steps wearily toward the house. The door, closing, sounded emptily in the big living room. He stood there, knowing without looking that Gay, too, was gone.

Rode off to town, he thought dully. He sagged down into an overstuffed chair, feeling suddenly empty inside, feeling very old.

He needed Gay—he needed her around. He stared dully around the big room. Gay was like Margaret, his wife; her presence made the big house less lonely.

But she was marrying soon! He remembered that now. She was marrying Walter Burke, a newcomer to Sundown. An attorney from back East —a suave, cultivated man Big Bill held in curiously mingled contempt and awe.

The big room weighed on him with its emptiness. Sitting there, his thoughts kept circling back to Bob, to the look in his son's eyes. He had had contempt for his son's weakness, but in this bitter moment he wished Bob had pulled that trigger!

He had driven his boys unmercifully, driven them harder than he had driven his hired hands. What had he been trying to prove?

He got up and walked to the kitchen. The bottle of whiskey was up on the shelf where he kept it. He took it down. . . .

An hour later he walked out to the veranda. Belk, one of the men he kept by the main gate, was just riding into the yard.

Big Bill called him over.

"Dab's out there somewhere," he said. "Down by the creek. Find him." Big Bill's breath reeked of whiskey, but his voice was steady, and curiously mild. "Belk—tell Dab it's all right. Tell him I want him to come home."

Bob Houseman rode slowly, keeping the sorrel to a walk. He was in no hurry to go anywhere. He was headed in the general direction of Sundown, and he had enough money in his pockets to enable him to take the stage to Wilson. His thoughts, when they moved in that direction, went that far and stopped. He had no particular plans, but there was a lightness in him, a feeling of relief that was as heady as strong drink.

He was his own man at last! And all it had taken was a stand, a final facing up to the man who had browbeat him through towering strength and acid contempt since he had grown to manhood.

He heard the horse's frantic whinnying first; then he became aware of the sickening scene below him. Bob's stomach tightened into a cold knot.

He had crested a small pocket, west of the tiny creek that ran through the H Bar H's north range.

A big, hammerheaded black horse was tied to a small jackpine. Short-reined to the tree, unable to jerk its head more than two or three inches, the black was plunging from side to side, whinnying with stricken fear.

Methodically, with sadistic brutalness, Dab Houseman was beating his cayuse with a club!

Bob's lips flattened against his teeth. It was not the first time he had caught his brother maltreating animals, and each time the sight had shocked him because of its unreasoning cruelty.

He rode down into that hot, still pocket, the sound of his coming smothered by the terror-stricken screams of the horse. Not until he slid from saddle and ran to Dab, gripping his brother's upraised arm, did Dab turn a dull, thick-lipped face to see who was interfering.

Bob felt the enormous strength in that thick, corded arm. He thrust his weight against it, yelling in Dab's ear: "You clumsy, thick-witted animal. I told you I'd rawhide you if I ever saw you beat another horse—"

He was older than Dab by five years, and he had always been able to cow his brother. He jerked at the club, tearing it from Dab's loosening fingers. "I oughta use this on yore thick skull!" he raged. He shook the club in front of Dab's unblinking, flat gray eyes. Dab backed away slowly, shaking his head, his thick lips working, uttering small garbled cries. Emotion did that to Dab Houseman: rendered him inarticulate.

Bob flung the club aside. "Go on, go home!" he cried angrily. There had never been anything between him and his brother. Dab worshipped his father like a dumb animal—and like a dumb animal he feared him. He was big and strong, like his father, and he wanted his father's admiration— but he used his strength against helpless animals, beating them with a deliberate cruelty that somehow compensated, in his thick, slow mind, for the need locked deep inside him.

Dab blinked his eyes then, like a shaggy bear. "Can't," he strangled. "Paw—he's mad—"

Bob took a deep breath. There was something piteous in Dab's eyes, a naked flash of fear mingled with a mute despair. He felt his gorge rise. He knew that he was responsible for Dab's plight. He had talked Dab into leaving, knowing how his father would feel.

"Come on," he said, erasing the anger from his voice. "I'll ride home with you."

Dab backed away, shaking his head. "Can't," he repeated thickly.

Bob's temper grated. "Can't you understand?" he yelled with the confidence of an older brother who had always been obeyed. "I said yo're goin' home—"

He stopped, his eyes widening with a stricken, horrible surprise.

Dab Houseman had picked up the club. He was snarling, "Can't—can't" as he lunged at his brother.

Bob threw up his right hand. But the club came down with the enormous power of Dab's shambling shoulders. The pine limb cracked Bob's forearm, broke in two, and drove Bob down to his hands and knees. Dab hit him with the shortened end, bashing in the base of Bob's head, driving his brother's face into the sand. He kept striking until the club was a broken, useless thing in his huge fist. . . .

For a long moment he stood, looking down at the bloody figure at his feet. Then he backed away, shaking his head like a bear trying to rid himself of a buzzing tormentor.

"Can't," he muttered.

He stood uncertainly, eyeing the big sorrel that stood ground-reined just beyond. He couldn't go home now. The thought penetrated his mind, lodged there unshakably.

The sorrel snorted as he shuffled up, gathered up the reins and swung into saddle. Some quirk in the depths of his twisted mind turned him toward the black. He rode alongside the quivering animal, loosened the reins. Wrapping them around his thick right arm, he rode out of the pocket.

Two hours later, still leading the black, he topped a rock-strewn slope that slanted north toward the foothills. He drew back with the wary instinct of an animal as a rider came into view on the faint thread of trail far below.

Slowly he licked his thick lips. He unloosened the reins from around his arm, forgetting the black in his eagerness to get at the rifle under his leg. The black backed away, shook its head at this sudden freedom, and broke into a run for the distant H Bar H range.

Dab leveled his rifle before he realized the range was too great. A snarl writhed his lips. Once before he had had this man in his sights. The scene unwound itself in his mind—the hot stillness of Homer's yard where a big brindle dog had cowered under his clubbing blows before the rider on the trail below had intruded.

Slowly he slid the rifle back into its scabbard. The rider had disappeared between huge rocks. But Dab Houseman knew where he was headed. This trail led to the Lazy L, Nate Beals' place.

He backed the sorrel away from the rim, his eyes glittering with animal cunning. This time the man who had diverted him from the brindle would not get away.

CHAPTER 11

The immense bulk of Paler's Peak shouldered the sky ahead of Jerry Lannigan, blotting out most of the horizon. The foothills were bare and rocky, fading into a long, spiny ridge that extended like a bony finger from the mountain's towering bulk.

The Lazy L was located in a small valley in the foothills.

Jerry reined in, taking a long look at the ramshackle buildings in the narrow valley. Half of the main house was of stone, An L of hewn logs connected it with the galley, from which the long, narrow bunkhouse made another L. It was constructed somewhat like a fort, and Jerry remembered that this was an old spread, and that the man who had built it had been here when marauding bands of Crow Indians had raided past Paler's Peak.

A man came out of the bunkhouse as he watched, moving across the yard to the ranchhouse. His back was to Jerry.

The deputy reached in his pocket for the makings. The badge glittered under his fingers. He rolled his smoke and lighted it, cupping the match between his hands.

He had come to let the Lazy L know that there was still law in the valley of the Jay; he wanted to get Nate Beals straight on that point. He dropped his hand, loosening the Colt that rode his thigh, before he sent the roan toward the buildings.

A long way up on the rocky slope overlooking the small valley, a thick-bodied figure slid a rifle across a small boulder and cursed softly. . . .

The man crossing the yard stopped at the foot of the ranchhouse steps and looked back as Jerry rode into the yard. He tensed, his right hand coming up slowly, thumb hooking in his sagging cartridge belt.

"I see the sheriff made yuh a deppity," he

sneered. "Yo're ridin' a little wide of yore stampin' grounds, ain't yuh?"

Jerry reined in a few feet from the Lazy L foreman. He didn't look around, but he sensed that men came to the door of the bunkhouse.

"The valley's my stamping ground," he said bleakly. "And the law's my business. Where's Nate Beals?"

Reo Cates hesitated. He glanced past Jerry to the bunkhouse door, where a slim man was slowly sliding a Colt from his holster. His lips curled. "I reckon yo're pushin' that badge too far, son. You should have—"

"Red!" Beals' voice snapped across that yard. "Darn it, man, we've had enough trouble with the law! Put up that Colt!"

He had come out as Reo talked, a big, dark man on the steps. The slim man he had called Red glanced at Cates. The foreman shrugged.

Beals' voice was rough. "I'm still bossin' this outfit, Jerry. Come inside and have your say. Cates —get the rest of the boys in here, too." His voice carried a hint of a sneer. "Maybe the law has something you ought to hear."

Jerry slid down from the roan. "I have got a few things to say, Nate," he said levelly. "First, though, I want Link Ellers!"

Nate stiffened. He peered at Jerry, a scowl pushing across his scarred face. "Ellers is in a cell, in Sundown," he growled. "What's yore game, Jerry?"

If he was acting, Jerry thought, the man was awfully good at it.

"Someone killed Joe Semper and turned Link loose," Jerry said evenly. "Far as I know only the Lazy L would want Ellers free."

Beals shook his head. He looked at Cates, smiling thinly, at the men straggling out of the bunkhouse. A hard crew—he had hired them because of that fact. Now he felt misgivings. It was not a new feeling. It had been growing on him since before that night in the bar across the river in Sundown.

He was the boss, but Cates gave the orders here.

"I haven't seen Ellers since you hauled him out of the Lone Star," he snapped. "None of my men have been to town since." He scowled. "You're nosing up the wrong tree, Jerry."

Reo Cates glanced at the bunkhouse. His men had come soft-footed to stand beside him. The bunkhouse loomed empty.

Jerry studied Cates' face. It was a long, hard face, made even tougher by the small white scar across the base of his hawk nose. And looking at the Lazy L ramrod, he was certain that Cates knew about Ellers—that Cates knew a lot of things Nate Beals didn't.

He remembered Sheriff Stevens' suspicions then. The old lawman had had a hunch that the real trouble in the valley was not going to be that between Houseman and Beals. . . .

"I came up to tell you about Ellers, Nate," Jerry said coldly. "And to warn you. If you didn't break that killer out, then someone—"

Only Beals and Cates saw the man who appeared in the bunkhouse door. A thin man, his right arm wrapped in a dirty, blood-stained bandage. He was holding a Colt in his left hand.

Beals stiffened. "Ellers!"

Jerry whirled. His fingers were closing over his

gun butt when Link's slug scraped the top of his shoulder, spun him off balance. He saw Cates' move, felt the man bend toward him. Then Cates' gunside slammed against Jerry's head, sent him sprawling, face down, in the dust of the Lazy L ranchyard.

Beals was standing on the top step, staring at the figure who came toward him. Link was levelling a gun at Jerry's unconscious body. . . .

Nate came down the steps in one jump. He thrust his big frame against Cates, spinning the foreman aside, and confronted the straw-haired killer. "So you were here all the time," he said harshly. "Hiding out in my bunkhouse—"

Link's gun tilted. The shot stopped Nate Beals. A great surprise widened his eyes. His mouth moved, but no sound came from between his lips.

Link sneered as he fell, sliding limply across Jerry Lannigan's still form.

Cates was grinning coldly. "The silly fool!" he whispered softly. "He actually thought he was runnin' this show."

Link stepped to the sprawled figures and looked

down at Jerry. His thumb was hauling back the hammer of his Colt when Cates shoved him away.

"He'll keep," the dark-faced ramrod said. "Let's hold him over for the boss!"

Link shrugged. One of the men bent over Beals, turned the man over. "Well!" he said disgustedly. "Yuh can't shoot a darn with yore left hand, Link. The big boy's still alive!"

Cates grinned. "Take 'em inside the house, boys. I'm figgerin' the boss'll be plumb surprised when he shows up!"

The stagecoach into Wilson dropped off two passengers that night. One was a dumpy, middle-aged woman, visiting relatives. The other was Lawyer Burke.

All the way in from Sundown he had sat in morose silence. His jaw was slightly swollen, his lower lip was puffed.

He picked up his handbag and started walking toward the railroad station. He walked rapidly, his tall, lean, neatly dressed figure merging into the shadows. He turned right at the small depot.

Ahead of him the iron rails glinted faintly, heading into the black immensity past the town.

The lights of Wilson fell behind as he walked. The cinders crunched under his feet. He went past a small, dark toolshed and turned down a faintly discernible path that led off the railway embankment.

Water made a soft, whispering sound in the darkness. The attorney turned toward it. The two men waiting by the trickle of water turned to him. "Nick?" The voice was a sibilant whisper.

The attorney from Sundown grunted. "Where's the horses, Mike?"

Mike loomed up, a heavy-shouldered shadow. His companion dropped his cigaret and ground it under his heel.

"Down in the gully," Mike answered.

Nick Shard, who had posed as Lawyer Walter Burke, unsnapped his handbag. From inside the bag he took out a black shirt, a black pair of pants, black leather boots and a black bag. A pair of matched Colts, encased in their holsters, were the last items in the bag.

There, in the darkness beyond the steel rails, Lawyer Burke shed his identity as easily as he shed his town clothes. The man who turned to Mike was a lean, deadly figure—a man who was wanted by the sheriff of half a dozen counties north of the valley of the Jay. Nick Shard—wanted for rustling, bank robbery and murder!

"Let's move," he said harshly. "We've got an all night ride ahead of us!"

CHAPTER 12

The sun flushed the horizon clouds. Daylight pushed back the shadows from the H Bar H; slowly the buildings took on outline in the strengthening light. A chicken hawk swooped low on noiseless wings over the still yard, banked for a return trip and suddenly winged upward as a horseman rode slowly into the yard. He was a stiff-backed figure, tired from an all night search. Across his saddle a slim body was doubled in grotesque stiffness.

Big Bill came out to the veranda as Belk dismounted.

He stood looking down at the body taking shape in the morning light. Belk said tiredly: "It's Bob.

Someone clubbed him to death." Belk's voice had a dry rasp. "He's not a pretty sight."

Big Bill stood rooted, a horrible suspicion crawling through his whiskey-numbed mind. "Where's Dab?"

Belk shrugged. He stood by the animal, a tall and rangy man, his shoulders bowed. "Warn't much light to read sign," he said dryly. "Found Bob in a small hollow, 'bout eight miles from here. North of the creek. His cayuse was gone. Whoever killed him rode Bob's hoss away, leadin' his own. I followed the tracks a ways before I turned back."

He was silent a moment, choosing his words. "The tracks headed for the Lazy L."

Big Bill licked dry lips. Belk's words gave him the lead he wanted—helped him down the ugly thought that had shaken him. Tired and beaten and faced with the bitter realization of the lonely years ahead, he suddenly wanted to vent his anger, his bitter frustration on something tangible.

"He said he'd make me pay!" he grated harshly. "Make me pay for that whippin' I gave him in

Sundown! This is Nate Beals' way of gettin' even!"

Belk said nothing. His tired animal moved restlessly with its unmoving burden.

Big Bill came down, his voice thin with suppressed hate. "I'll take Bob," he said. "Saddle up a cayuse for me an' a fresh one for yoreself. I'll be out in five minutes."

He waited until Belk moved away before lifting his hands to the still, cold figure across the saddle. Gently his big hands eased his son's body into his arms. After that first look at Bob's almost unrecognizable face he averted his gaze. He went up the stairs with his burden, into the lamplit living room where he had paced a weary vigil.

Gay had not come home. But often she went to town and stayed overnight at some friend's house.

He walked across the big room, down a short hallway to Bob's bedroom. The sun's first rays, coming through the window, fell across the bed. Slowly Big Bill laid the body down on the covers.

There would be time later, he thought, to bury Bob. A dull hate throbbed in him. Time later—

when he had settled things with Nate Beals!

He turned and walked out, his boots making a heavy, echoing sound in that empty room.

He waited on the veranda until Belk came up, riding a fresh cayuse and leading a long-legged roan.

Most of his men were with the herd he had been gathering for a drive to Wilson. It would take him several hours to get to them, and then a long ride to the Lazy L.

He shook the tiredness of the long night from his heavy shoulders as he whirled the roan, sent it lunging down the yard. . . .

Wood smoke drifted up from the Lazy L galley, a gray-blue smudge that hovered in the still morning. High up on the rocky slope overlooking the small valley Dab Houseman stirred and blinked his eyes. He had fallen asleep as he had lain prone, waiting with the patience of a hunting animal for Jerry Lannigan to leave. Sometime during the night he had rolled over; he was staring up into the lightening sky when he awoke.

He turned quickly, coming erect like some shambling bear. Moving up the slope a couple of feet, he settled himself patiently.

No one had left the valley below during the night, he was positive of that. The man he wanted would have to come out sometime. From his position, the flurry of action in front of the ranchhouse had been too far to distinguish in detail.

His attention shifted to the entrance to the valley, narrowing on the three riders moving toward the buildings at a steady jog. Disappointment glinted briefly in his eyes.

He recognized none of the newcomers. Slowly he settled back to wait. . . .

Reo Cates came into the ranchhouse through the galley, holding a mug between his palms. The man who had built the Lazy L had been content to eat with his hired help, and the dining room connected both the main house and the bunkhouse. Nate Beals, however, had had the cook bring him his meals into the big room that served as both living and sleeping quarters.

Cates teetered slightly on his toes, his dark face

impassive. "Any trouble, Red?" he asked softly.

Red Venters, sitting at the big table by the stone fireplace, shook his head. He had his eyes glued to the cards spread out before him, solitaire fashion. A pearl-handled Colt was also on the table, near his right hand.

"Meek as a lamb, Reo," he answered carelessly. "Ain't heard a peep out of him all night."

The Lazy L ramrod sipped at his coffee. His dark glance went to Jerry Lannigan, sitting on the floor, his back propped against the far wall. The deputy's hands and feet were securely bound. Cates' gaze shifted to the man breathing raggedly on the horsehair sofa. There had been no need to tie Beals, he thought callously. He was surprised the man had lived through the night.

He caught the flicker of Jerry's eyes and he walked to the bound man, chuckling softly. "Walked right into it, like a chuckle-headed fool," he sneered. "Wearin' a deppity's badge like you thought it was sacred."

Jerry's eyes met his, cold and bright. Link's bullet had ploughed a ragged furrow across the top of his shoulder. The cut had bled enough to stain the back of his shirt.

"Tough Jerry Lannigan!" Reo mocked. "Yeah —Nate talked about you. Grew up here, in the Crescent," he said. "Used to be sweet on Houseman's gal, too." Reo seemed to find something very funny in this. "Quite a gal, thet yaller-haired woman," he sneered. "Playful skirt, from what I hear."

Red swept the cards into a pile and snorted disgustedly. He got up, yawning. "Boss oughta get here soon," he muttered. "I been tired of playin' cowhand for days." He reached down for the Colt, automatically checked it before sliding it back into holster.

Reo moved away from Jerry. "We move today," he promised. "Sykes came back last night from scoutin' the H Bar H. The fools are doin' our jobs for us. 'Bout eighteen hundred head, mostly three years old, waitin' for us."

Red nodded. "I been gettin' old jest sittin' around here listenin' to him talk." He jerked his head to the dying man. "All the time he was makin' his plans to buck Houseman, we been making ours." He walked to the window and glanced outside. "Haven't seen Davis or Whitey in near a week, Reo."

The ramrod shrugged. "If they're doin' what they were told, they're scarin' the daylights out of the Akers family. We don't want anyone within hearin' distance when we herd them H Bar H cattle through the Wall."

Red yawned again. "Aw be quiet!" he growled. "Reckon I'll go into the galley for a cup of—" He bent closer to the window, peering out. "Looks like the boss ridin' in, Reo," he muttered. "Yep, it's Nick. Mike an' Pecos are with him."

Cates turned to Lannigan. His eyes glittered with silent mirth. "Looks like you an' the boss will be mutually surprised. Yeah," he added, suddenly chuckling. "Plumb surprised!"

Jerry Lannigan sat very still, his back pressed against the wall. The ache in his shoulder had long since spread to his arms and back. In the beginning he had tried to loosen the rope that bound his wrists, and his silent, grim effort had only served to awaken a grudging admiration for the man who had tied him.

His eyes strayed to Beals. Jerry had no recollection of what had happened after Cates slugged him. When he had come to he had found himself propped where he now was, securely tied. Beals was on the sofa. But he had heard enough to understand that Ellers had shot Nate when the Lazy L boss had tried to interfere.

Jerry closed his eyes for a brief instant. When he opened them Cates was moving back from the door. "Got a surprise for yuh, Nick," the ramrod was saying. "Come on in."

A tall man in dusty black clothes stepped inside, pausing to search the room with frowning regard. Sagging cartridge belts crossed at his flat waist, the holsters tied down at his thighs.

Jerry suddenly jerked forward. There were tired lines in that man's face, and he needed a shave —but despite this, and the dusty range clothes, the deputy from Sundown recognized him. Attorney Walter Burke—the man who was going to marry

Gay Houseman!

The whole pattern of trouble suddenly made sense to Jerry Lannigan. Stevens' tired voice whispered in his ears. *The big trouble, when it comes, won't be between Houseman an' Beals!*

From the beginning Beals' men had taken the play away from him. Charley's killing had been a deliberate play by Ellers to suck the sheriff and his deputy into a gun trap, to wipe out the law in Sundown.

Beals had hired these men, and paid them gunman wages—but someone else had given them orders. A smooth-talking, suave man who had come to Sundown and passed himself off as a lawyer—a man who had quickly sized up the situation in the valley and used the brewing trouble between Nate and Big Bill Houseman to advance his own ends.

Nick Shard, alias Walter Burke, was stepping across the room, a crooked smile twisting his lips. "I was hoping you'd follow me," he said coldly. "I staged that ride to Wilson for your benefit. I wanted you to come after me. But this is better."

He turned to Cates. "When'd he get in, Reo?"

"Last night," Reo said. He gave Nick the details in terse monosyllables. "Ellers shot Nate. The fool was beginnin' to get in our way."

The phony lawyer began to laugh. It was a cold and grating sound, with little mirth. "Fine," he muttered. "It all ties in neatly." He turned as the rest of the Lazy L crew shuffled in.

Link Ellers smiled briefly. "Neatest bit of jail breakin' I ever saw, boss," he said admiringly. "Joe died before he knew what hit him." ˙

Red Venters growled: "I been spendin' my cut of that herd money for a week, boss. When we gonna ride?"

Nick was looking down at Jerry, frowning thoughtfully. "Reo?" he said softly. "You still have that half-case of dynamite?"

Reo nodded. "Out in the shed."

"Get it," Nick said. He was grinning again. "Bring a fuse and a cap."

Reo shrugged. He pushed his way through the crowding men. Red muttered: "A bullet is quicker—"

Nick Shard swung on him. "You have any objections, Red?" His voice was thin, questioning.

Red scowled. But he kept his mouth shut.

Cates came back, lugging a small wooden case. The top had been pried open. Small round yellowish cylinders about six inches long were nestled in straw. Cates walked gingerly and slowly set the box down on the table. He turned to Nick.

The outlaw boss walked to the table, laid a hand on the case. He looked at Red. "You keep your mouth shut and listen, and maybe you'll get to spend your share of the herd money. Maybe even more." He made a small gesture with his hands, like a lawyer about to address a jury.

"Two of you will ride now, as we planned. You'll get close enough to the H Bar H ranchhouse to shoot a few holes in the windows. If either of Houseman's boys are around, shoot to kill! I want Big Bill to know it's the Lazy L who did it! I want him so blind mad he'll pull that hard crew away from those cows and come up here for a shootout!"

He paused, waiting for the effect of his words

on those men. Once he had studied law—once he had been Walter Burke. But that was ten years ago—before he had become Nick Shard, outlaw.

"The rest of you head for the herd. Hole up where you can see what happens. If things work out the way they should, Big Bill will be riding this way before nightfall."

One of the men shifted, a puzzled frown over his eyes. "What happens when the H Bar H finds no one here, except—?" He glanced at Jerry and then at Beals.

Nick Shard tapped the case of dynamite. "This," he said shortly. He nodded at Ellers. "Link will be here, waiting. We'll set a fifteen minute fuse to this stuff."

Link started to protest. Nick cut him short. "With that arm you'll be in the way with the herd."

Reo Cates nodded, a light of understanding in his eyes. "Link can spot them comin' up the valley long enough to touch a match to the fuse an' slip out the back door. Houseman's riders should be close enough by the time the whole buildin' goes up to get spattered all over the yard!"

Nick nodded. "It'll take a long time for some-one to untangle what happened. We'll be a long way from here by then. A long way."

He moved away from the table, his voice sud-denly crisp. "Ellers stays. Reo, I want you to ride to Sundown with me. The rest of you saddle up. "You're riding now!"

He walked to the door, Cates beside him, and waited until the last of them had gone.

"I thought we were leavin' the valley," Cates said.

"We are," Nick said. "We'll leave it clean—and broke!" He turned, looking back to Jerry Lanni-gan. "I'd like to be here when Link lights that fuse," he said. "I'd like to see your face—"

He turned to the thin-faced gunster with the bandaged arm. "We'll see you on the other side of the Wall, Link. Some time around noon, to-morrow."

Cates turned for one last look at Lannigan be-fore he followed Nick Shard outside. Link Ellers was settling back in a chair, a thin, bleak smile on his narrow face.

Jerry Lannigan eased back against the wall, fighting a feeling of hopeless desperation. There was nothing he could do, except wait!

CHAPTER 13

Dab Houseman waited patiently, a deep puzzlement wrinkling his forehead. Eight riders had left the Lazy L—and fifteen minutes later two others had come out of the house and ridden off. The man he wanted had not been among them.

It was more than half an hour since the last riders had departed. There had been, since then, no sign of life in the small valley below.

Curiosity wormed its way through Dab Houseman's clogged brain. The man was down there, in that big house. He had been carried inside, and he had not come out.

Slowly he crawled back from the rim.

It took him almost an hour to find his way down into that narrow valley, to come shambling up behind the galley. He stopped, his rifle clutched in one thick hand, and listened.

A man was talking, but he couldn't make out words; only the blurred tones filtered out to him. Then the wind, shifting direction, brought the faint, far sound of gunfire.

He flattened against the galley wall, shaking his head from side to side like a puzzled animal. The voice stopped talking.

The gunfire faded. Dab Houseman moved along the galley wall until he found a door. It opened to his hand. He waited, listening intently. Somewhere inside a man was breathing with a raspy, jerky sound.

He shuffled into the galley. Past the wood stove and the long benches flanking a wooden table he could see into another room. Dab blinked his eyes. He could see the back of a man's head and shoulders—a slim man with a bandaged right arm. The man was standing, looking down at another, sitting with his back to the far wall.

A slow, pleased grin broke across Dab's face. him. He shuffled toward the room, lifting his rifle up across his thick waist.

Jerry Lannigan saw the man loom up behind Link. For a moment hope flickered crazily through him. Then he saw the look in Dab's eyes, saw the rifle muzzle swing in line with him, and he threw himself sideways, twisting away from the wall.

Dab's rifle cracked a split second later.

Link whirled. He had his Colt stuck in his belt, within easy reach of his left hand. He saw Dab's hulking figure in the galley doorway, levering another shell into firing position, and he shot by instinct.

The .45 slug should have knocked the man down. It didn't. Dab staggered, turned to face the man who had shot him. Ellers shot again. Panic sent his third shot wide.

Dab Houseman shuffled toward him, lifting the rifle like a club over his head. Ellers emptied his gun into that broad target before Dab hit him. Link fell against the wall, the right side of his face spurting blood. Dab swung the rifle methodically, his breath coming in huge, wheezing gasps.

Finally Dab Houseman stopped. He swayed on his feet, turning slowly, his eyes glazed. He saw Jerry Lannigan on the floor. He saw the deputy through a red haze. There was a great roaring in his head, an unsteadiness in his legs.

Slowly, with ponderous effort, he raised the rifle over his head!

Jerry rolled violently. He kept rolling, trying to get away from the crazy man who stalked him, slowly, with upraised rifle.

The sofa stopped him. He tried to get his legs under him at that last moment, to lash out with them in desperate effort to ward off that clubbing blow.

Dab stopped. He loomed over Jerry, his face a twisted gargoyle. The entire front of his shirt was a bloody mess.

Jerry heard it then, the sound of riders sweeping up to the house. He heard voices call sharply. Then boots thudded on the steps, the door burst open to the shouldering of hard-eyed men.

"Dab!" Big Bill's voice lashed into the room.

Dab Houseman's thick shoulders jerked, as though a shot had slammed between them. He turned his head to the man coming into the room. Fear twisted nakedly across his broad features. "Can't!" he mumbled. He backed away as Big Bill came toward him. "Can't go home—no more!"

His boot heel caught Jerry's outstretched leg. He teetered; then the strength seemed to go out of him in one sudden rush. He fell across Jerry's legs.

Big Bill stared at the shambles in the room, his eyes uncomprehending. Beals was groaning. The fracas must have penetrated through his fogged mind. He turned, tried to push himself up to a sitting position. He saw Big Bill through blurred, pained eyes, and hate choked one final bitter oath from him.

"Damn you, Houseman! I'll be waiting for you —in hell!"

Big Bill didn't look at Nate—didn't seem to hear him. He was looking down at Dab, a big, broken man, his hands by his sides, a Colt still gripped in his right one. A half-dozen grim-faced H Bar H riders clustered around him.

Jerry took a deep breath. "Never thought I'd be this happy to see you, Bill. Cut me loose before I change my mind."

Big Bill knelt beside him, thrusting a hand into his pocket. He found a clasp knife and used it, cutting Jerry free.

The deputy sat up, working his fingers, trying to get the blood back through his wrists. His feet were numb, unfeeling at first; then they began to pain as though pricked by a thousand needles.

Big Bill was bending over his son. Dab was dead.

After a long, still moment he straightened.

One of his men muttered: "Nate Beals is dead. There's another corpse by the wall." He ended with a slow, puzzled whistle.

Jerry got to his feet. "I don't know why he wanted to kill me, Bill," he said, nodding to Dab's body. "But he came in here looking for me. He came in through the galley, and I saw his eyes when he saw me. He was looking for me, Bill. Why? Did you send him?"

Big Bill shook his head. "I haven't seen Dab

since yesterday." He told Jerry what had happened, told him about finding Bob. "I reckon I knew all along that Dab had killed Bob," he said. His voice was low, tired. "But I didn't want to believe it. I wanted to think it was the Lazy L—I wanted to settle things with Nate once and for all—"

Jerry nodded. "Then Dab must have followed me here on his own." He frowned. "I wonder why, Bill. I only saw him once, since I've been back."

Big Bill shrugged. "I don't know. He had his own reasons for the things he did." He turned wearily, sagged his bulk into a chair.

For a brief moment there came to Jerry then the sharp recollection of a dog tied to a stake in Homer's yard; he felt again the prickle down his spine as a hidden rifleman watched him from the rocks above the small clearing.

Big Bill said: "I reckon it's all over, Jerry." There was no note of triumph in his voice, no emotion whatever. "We ran into most of the Lazy

L up in the hills. They looked like they were headed for my range—they seemed plumb surprised to see us!" He shook his head. "We wiped them out—to the man, Jerry!"

Lannigan remembered then the two men heading for Sundown. Two men, the worst of the lot.

There was no time to explain to Big Bill the pawn Nate Beals had been in this trouble. At the moment Big Bill wouldn't have cared.

"Not quite all, Bill," he answered grimly. "There's one man I want—want badly!" He reached down in an instinctive gesture to his empty holster. There was no time to waste looking for his gun. Reaching out, he took Big Bill's Colt from the big man's hand.

"I'll give it back to you, Bill," he promised. "After I use it—on your daughter's fiancé!"

He was across the room, clumping down the steps, before Big Bill caught the meaning of his words.

H Bar H horses crowded the rail. Jerry picked out the fastest-looking animal, a big blue roan. He had a long way to go, and he knew he'd never catch up with Cates and Nick Shard.

But if the big roan held out, he'd be there before they left Sundown!

CHAPTER 14

A high wind was blowing off Paler's Peak, sending great cloud puffs sailing across the cobalt sky.
The shadow patterns moved across the valley, sliding noiselessly over the surface of the land.

Reo Cates spat over his horse's left ear. "There
it is, Nick," he said. "Ready for the pickin'!"

Sundown sprawled along the Jay, windows reflecting the slanting sun. A peaceful town, a settled
town. That was how Sundown first appeared to
the stranger.

Nick Shard pulled his mount off the road toward a nest of boulders. Reo followed him. He
waited, slouched in saddle, while the outlaw boss
took down his leather bag which he had tied to his

horse's cantle; watched with impassive eyes while Nick divested himself of his dusty black clothes, replaced them with the somewhat wrinkled town clothes he had worn to Wilson.

Cates grinned briefly as Nick buckled on the twin cartridge belts, checked his guns. "Seems more natural when you wear them, boss," he said.

Nick patted the skirts of his long coat over the holsters. "With Stevens laid up, and his deputy taken care of, we won't run into trouble with the law. But the bank teller might object." The phony lawyer grinned coldly. "Just in case, Reo," he said, sliding his hands over the bulges under his coat.

He secured the leather grip on his cantle, and swung into saddle. He looked up at the westering sun, and slid his hand along his watch chain. "You'll need this," he said to Cates. He handed him the gold watch. "The bank closes at four. Remember, there's a five minute fuse on that dynamite I've planted under the bridge. Wait until quarter of four; then touch a match to the fuse, and get out of there in a hurry. I'll meet you by the bend in the creek, about an hour later."

Reo nodded. He hung back, waiting until Nick Shard was a small far figure on the road to Sundown. Then he rode slowly after him. He quit the road a mile from town, circling until he hit the gully that ran into the Jay. He disappeared into this fold of earth and dismounted.

Instinctively he glanced at the sun, before dragging out the watch Nick had given him. Five minutes to three. He had a little more than three quarters of an hour to kill.

He settled his lanky frame against the gully side and started to build himself a smoke. . . .

Nick Shard rode slowly into town. Coming from the north, he had to ride through the squalid, newer section across the bridge. He sat loosely in saddle, thinking of the role he had played in this town. A role he had been able to carry off because once he had studied law. Thinking about it now, it seemed long ago—part of a hazy and remote past.

His horse pounded on the bridge planks, booming hollowly in the afternoon stillness. He turned right on River Road, and when he came to his office he dismounted.

Harry Meeker who owned the haberdashery next door greeted him pleasantly. "Glad to see you back, Walter. Heard you'd taken the stage to Wilson."

Nick nodded. "Business," he explained briefly. "Didn't take long—and I decided not to wait for the return stage."

He pushed through his door and closed it behind him. There was nothing of value to him in this office, nothing he wanted to take along when he left Sundown. The books, the furniture—these were only props, useful for the role he had played here.

Perhaps because he was thinking this way, Gay Houseman came into his thoughts. Her picture was on his desk. He looked at it steadily, a thin smile lengthening his lips.

She had been a prop, like his books and his furniture—like this office had been. She had completed the picture he had painted here. Now there was no longer need for the props. In less than an hour he would be leaving Sundown—leaving the valley of the Jay.

The eight day wall clock was still running. He glanced at it, suddenly impatient. Quarter after three.

He turned and walked out and stood on the walk before the office, looking down the road toward the bridge. He could stand a drink, he thought. He rubbed the back of his knuckles across his jaw, and the tenderness suddenly reminded him of Jerry Lannigan.

It occurred to him, with thin satisfaction, that it would be about this time that Link would be lighting the fuse to that half-case of dynamite.

There was a bar down the street, a block from the bank. He walked to it, pushed through the slatted doors.

There were two customers in the place, one of them dead drunk and sleeping noisily, slumped across a rear table. The other, a slight man with a cast in one eye, was arguing with the bartender.

Nick waited while the man behind the bar disengaged himself from the argument and came toward him. "Hear about Joe Semper gettin' killed?"

he asked, sliding a bottle and a glass to Nick. He went on without bothering to hear Nick's answer. Joe Semper's death had provided him with a topic of conversation and an outlet for his opinions which he proceeded to dispense freely.

"Used to be this town was peaceful, Mr. Burke. I been here fifteen years, an' I never had trouble in my place that I couldn't handle with my bung-starter. Now, with that gang that's been hangin' around across the river, I been keepin' a Colt under the counter."

"Good idea," Nick said absently. The whiskey was raw, but it gave him the edge he wanted.

"What we need in town, Mr. Burke, is a man who's handy with a gun." The bartender leaned on his elbows, his voice lowering confidentially. "In my opinion the sheriff's gettin' too old for this job. We need a man who kin make them hoodlums across the river toe the line. Somebuddy who ain't afraid of layin' down the law to Big Bill Houseman an' to Nate Beals, too. They're the cause of all the trouble we been havin', importin' gunmen like—"

"Maybe Sundown needs a man like Jerry Lannigan," Nick murmured. "He's wearing a deputy's star."

The bartender frowned. "He's a hard one, all right," he conceded. "But I remember him when he lived up in the Crescent, with old Jed Lafreau. He was a wild one in those days. I heard he changed after he left the valley. But if I was Sheriff Stevens—"

Nick plunked change on the counter, cutting the man short. "I don't trust him either," he said, straight-faced.

The wall clock ticked loudly in the momentary silence. It was time to go. He finished his drink and turned away.

He turned down the walk, his step leisurely. He didn't see the girl who was just stepping out of the dress shop, half a block behind him. He paused by the bank window, glanced inside. He could see the teller moving behind his cage; there was no one else inside the bank.

Instinctively his hands rubbed down over the Colt butts under his coat skirts. . . .

Behind him Gay Houseman, recognizing the tall

figure, opened her mouth to hail him. Her voice was drowned out in the sudden, rumbling roar that shook the town.

Gay looked back along River Road to where the bridge had straddled the Jay. Smoke shrouded the near bank of the river; debris from the blasted bridge was falling over town.

For a moment the surprise of the explosion held her. People were popping out of doors, heading for the bridge. She turned to see if Walter, too, was coming along the street, but his tall figure had disappeared.

Gay Houseman started to run toward the bank. . . .

Nick Shard stepped across the threshold, into the coolness of the bank interior, at the moment of the dynamiting of the bridge. The teller was starting out of his cage, drawn by the heavy, window-rattling sound. He saw Nick and pulled up, his eyes bright with excitement.

"Hear that, Mr. Burke? Sounded as though someone blew up—"

He backed up, his eyes widening, going muddy with fear. "Mr. Burke!" he said. His voice was sort of clogged in his throat. "Mr. Burke!" he repeated senselessly.

Nick made a motion with the muzzle of his drawn Colt. "Get inside that cage, Chris. I want everything you have in that safe. *Everything*. Put it in one of those canvas sacks you use to send to Wilson. Hurry!"

Chris' fingers fumbled with the greenbacks. He stuffed the money into the sack. Several bills fluttered to the floor, and he jerked a frightened glance at the cold-eyed man on the other side of the window.

He was thrusting the bulging sack under the wire grill when Gay Houseman came through the doorway!

Nick whirled, his gun levelling swiftly; his thumb held back the falling hammer by a hair's breadth.

Gay froze. She could see the bag in Walter's hand, see the white face of the teller behind the grillwork—but it didn't make sense to her. She couldn't believe what she was seeing.

The teller made his mistake, then. Perhaps he, too, couldn't quite believe that this man he had known as Attorney Burke would be capable of murder. At any rate, without the threat of the gun on him, he turned and made a break for the rear door.

Nick whirled. He thumbed two shots that sent Chris sprawling, tumbling inertly.

Gay screamed. It was a short cry, muffled by the instinctive blotting of her mouth with the back of her hand.

Nick strode to her, his face a dark, cold mask. "You walked in at the wrong time, Gay! Now you'll have to come with me!"

She shrank away, turned to run. He caught her arm, jerked her roughly around. "You empty-headed fool!" he sneered. "You played up to me, like you played up to every eligible man in the valley. But I was different—I was from back East, a lawyer." He laughed mockingly. "You fell for that. You—"

She tore out of his grasp, started to run for the

door. He caught her before she crossed the threshold. She went stiff, her eyes widening with terror, as he nudged her side with the muzzle of his Colt. "You make another break like that!" he grated, "and I'll kill you!"

She stood very still, while he drew a deep breath. "We're going out of here together. If anyone sees us—well, we were engaged to be married! My horse is in front of my office. You'll ride up behind me. *You understand?*"

Gay nodded wordlessly.

They went out together then. Out into the sun-splashed street that still held the rumbling echo of that blast that had destroyed the bridge!

Jerry Lannigan, pushing a wild-eyed, lathered blue roan, saw the bridge heave skyward, jagged pieces of timber spinning end over end, while he was still half a mile away. Seconds later the heavy burst of sound reached him.

He pulled off the road, his lips thinning against his teeth. Whatever Nick Shard had planned, Lannigan knew this was part of it. And he knew then that he had made Sundown in time.

The bridge was blown up, and the Jay, running deep between steep banks, was between him and the main section of town. But Jerry remembered a place where the river widened, where a horse might swim across.

He saw the rider pop up out of the gully ahead of him, less than a hundred yards away. He was headed in Jerry's direction, but he hauled back on his reins almost immediately, pulling his cayuse back on its haunches.

There was no time for wonder, no time even to break the running stride of the roan. He saw the man and knew he was Reo Cates—and then his hand was coming up, levelling Big Bill Houseman's Colt.

Cates drew and fired in one swift, desperate move. Jerry's lead knocked him out of saddle. He fell loosely, like a stuffed dummy; he was dead when he hit the ground.

Jerry kept riding. He turned the roan toward the Jay and sent it down into the current. The stallion plunged desperately, fighting the pull of the water. He made the shallows on the other side and hunched up the slope.

Grimly Jerry turned him toward town, sent him plunging past the first thin scatter of buildings along River Road.

He saw Nick and Gay come out of the bank ahead, head toward the blasted bridge. Surprise held him stiff-legged in his stirrups. He had not counted on Gay!

Nick turned to locate the rider. Jerry saw the shock that went through the man, the naked surprise that stamped itself on his thin, dark face. Gay, turning more slowly, suddenly uttered a glad cry.

Nick pulled her to him, his left hand sliding about her waist, shoving her in front of him. His Colt came up, but Gay's elbow was in the way.

The roan stiffened in its broken-strided run, went down with Nick's bullet through its heart. Jerry slipped free of the stirrups as the roan fell; he hit slightly off balance, fell forward on his hands and knees. The move saved his life.

Nick's second bullet whistled over his head.

Jerry stiffened. He had Big Bill's Colt in his fist.

But he couldn't use it. Gay was staring at him, white-faced, her body covering most of Nick. She wasn't fighting the man.

Nick's voice came sharply through the sudden stillness. "You've got more lives than a cat, Lannigan! But this time—"

Jerry tensed, gathering his muscles for a suicidal charge. It was no chance, yet it was his only hope.

The men coming up the street were too far away, and none of them was carrying a gun. He saw Nick's muzzle level, and he lunged up.

Sheriff Stevens killed Nick! From his window in Ma Jennings' boarding house, where he had come, attracted by the explosion.

Nick and Gay were almost directly below him. His bullet went through Nick's head, and killed him instantly.

Gay felt the loosening of Nick's arm. She twisted free then, turning a terrified gaze backward. She saw Nick slumping, his face a bloody mess.

She fainted.

Jerry caught her as she fell.

Two days later "Judge" Jenkins arrived on the stage from Wilson. Jerry met him at the stage office.

Jenkins looked around him. It was a sunny day, warm and drowsy. The waters of the Jay made a peaceful gurgling. Uptown, men were rebuilding the blasted bridge, the sound of their hammering seeming to underline the staid quiet of the town.

Jenkins scowled. "I came pronto, son," he said, "soon as I got yore wire." He looked around him again. "Danged if I see any sign of trouble!"

Jerry shrugged. He was still wearing Stevens' badge. But his roan was saddled, and waiting to ride.

"I'll tell you about it later."

Jenkins followed him, a tall man with a hard, cynical face. Jerry walked down the street to Ma Jennings' and went upstairs to Stevens' room. The sheriff was wearing an old robe thrown over his bony shoulders. He was sitting in a chair by the window.

Jenkins came in with Jerry and stood aside, watching the younger man. Lannigan walked up to

Stevens, his fingers reaching up, unpinning the badge.

"You need a deputy, Lafe," he said. His voice was level.

Stevens looked at Jenkins, standing by the door. Then his gaze came back to Jerry and his brows came together. "I've got one," he said sharply. "A good one!"

Jerry shook his head. "I'm leaving," he said flatly. "For good."

Stevens eyed him quietly. "We need you here, son."

Jerry's smile flickered across his lips. "Thanks, Lafe." He dropped the badge in the lawman's lap and walked back across the room, out through the door. Jenkins took a long look at Stevens before turning away.

Gay was waiting for him on the walk outside. She had come alone to town. She was dressed in black, but even in mourning she made men turn and look at her.

"Jerry," she said softly, ignoring the man behind Lannigan, "I waited for you to come to the ranch. When you didn't—I came to find you."

Lannigan looked at her—at this woman he had come back to marry. He had loved her when he was twenty, he had thought he loved her when he had come back. He was quite surprised to find that she meant so little to him now.

"Thanks for coming," he said. "Goodbye, Gay."

Her eyes were big in her face. She couldn't understand. "Jerry!"

He said softly: "Goodbye, Gay." He wheeled away then, with Jenkins falling in beside him. They walked silently to where Jerry had left Rebel.

"You'll have to buy a cayuse and saddle," Lannigan said. "I'm riding with you—to Wyoming."

Jenkins shrugged. They went into the livery stables and Jenkins made his choice. They rode out together.

"Where we going, son?" Jenkins asked once. They had crossed the floor of the valley and were heading through rocky hillocks.

"To the Broken Circle," Jerry said briefly.

"Where I grew up."

It was midafternoon when they pulled up in the small ranchyard. A big brindle dog came around the corner of a partly erected barn, barking a greeting to Jerry. A brown-faced boy of about ten followed him, his face breaking out into a wide smile.

The door in the house opened and Marion Akers stepped out. Her mother's thin face showed behind her.

Jerry said: "I've come to say goodbye, Marion."

Jenkins lifted his hand to rub his beard-roughened jaw, a thin light of understanding in his eyes. There was a boy and a woman here, and a man coming around the corner of the barn, a hammer in his hand. But Jerry was saying goodbye only to this girl on the veranda.

"You leaving?" she asked softly.

Jerry nodded. "Heading Wyoming way."

Her gaze shifted momentarily to Jenkins' impassive features. A smile touched her lips. "You can't go, Jerry!" Her voice had a determined ring to it.

Jerry stiffened slightly. "Why?"

Marion's smile was warm. "There's work to do here. The barn needs rebuilding. The corrals are in bad repair. Why, we can't do all the work. After all," she looked him squarely in the face, "this is your place, Jerry!"

He didn't say anything.

She added softly: "Sheriff Stevens told me yesterday."

Jenkins put a hand on Jerry's shoulder. "Reckon I'll be on my way, son," he said gruffly. His sharp-weathered face cracked in a smile. "This time I won't be expecting you—in Wyoming."

He turned to look back just before he crossed the Upper Jay. "Reckon the kid's finally found what he was lookin' for, hoss," he growled. "A mighty lucky man!"

He turned then and splashed across the creek, his broad back taking the beat of the westering sun.

THE END.

Peter B. Germano was born the oldest of six children in New Bedford, Massachusetts. During the Great Depression, he had to go to work before completing high school. It left him with a powerful drive to continue his formal education later in life, finally earning a Master's degree from Loyola University in Los Angeles in 1970. He sold his first Western story to A.A. Wyn's Ace Publishing magazine group when he was twenty years old. In the same issue of *Sure-Fire Western* (1/39) Germano had two stories, one by Peter Germano and the other by Barry Cord. He came to prefer the Barry Cord name for his Western fiction. When the Second World War came, he joined the U.S. Marine Corps. Following the war he would be called back to active duty, again as a combat correspondent, during the Korean conflict. In 1948 Germano began publishing a series of Western novels as Barry Cord notable for their complex plots while the scenes themselves are simply set, with a minimum of description and quick character sketches employed to establish a wide assortment of very different personalities. The pacing, which often seems swift due to the adept use of a parallel plot structure (narrating a story from several different viewpoints), is combined in these novels with atmospheric descriptions of weather and terrain. *Dry Range* (1955), *The Sagebrush Kid* (1954), *The Iron Trail Killers* (1960), and *Trouble in Peaceful Valley* (1968) are among his best Westerns. "The great southwest. . .," Germano wrote in 1982, "this is the country, and these are the people that gripped my imagination . . . and this is what I have been writing about for forty years. And until I die I shall remain the little New England boy who fell in love with the 'West,' and as a man had the opportunity to see it and live in it."

FIC
Cord

Cord, Barry, 1913-
Trail to Sundown / Barry Cord. --Bath, [England] :
Chivers Press, 1999, c1981.
220 p. --(Gunsmoke westerns)

954931   ISBN:075408048X

1. Western stories.   I. Title

503   99JUN10   ONF/v   1-567009